The Shark's Widow

Chris Maye was a good wife. When she learned that her loan-shark husband had been kidnapped, she followed instructions and came up with the ransom. But when she went to make the payoff, she discovered that she'd suddenly and brutally become a widow.

Ordinarily she would have gone to the police to find her husband's murderer, but this was a special case . . . a case she was willing to pay Mike Shayne $25,000 to handle . . . a case where only a private eye like Shayne could find the killer—*because in this case the killer was a cop.* . . .

Win Some, Lose Some

Brett Halliday

A DELL BOOK

Published by
Dell Publishing Co., Inc.
1 Dag Hammarskjold Plaza
New York, New York 10017

Dell ® TM 681510, Dell Publishing Co., Inc.
Printed in the United States of America
First printing—June 1976

Chapter 1

When the big highways came through downtown Miami, the old neighborhoods were ripped apart. Whole blocks were abandoned to the squatters and looters. Businesses failed or moved elsewhere.

Eddie Maye's saloon, in the shadow of the Interstate, no longer pumped enough beer to break even. Eddie kept it open because he needed the location. He had the loan-shark concession between North Miami Avenue and the waterfront, including the docks and warehouses of the Port of Miami. This end of his business, too, had been hurt by the changes. Few of the tenants in the new high-rises needed Eddie; in fact, they thought there was something demeaning and socially wrong about using a Shylock. Eddie was beginning to think there was an unfairness about the old territorial structure. He wanted to be allowed to pursue business, wherever it was.

Eddie was a popular man in a profession where it is easy to make enemies. Of course, there is no use pretending a Shylock is Santa Claus. People came to him only if they were sure they would be turned down everywhere else. The vigorish was higher than at a bank or a loan office, but the nature of the transaction was exactly the same. He loaned money expecting to get it back. Being a pretty fair judge of human nature, he generally managed to recover. Every lender, from the trap-mouthed, tight-assed personal-loan officer in the First National Bank, to Eddie Maye, the affable proprietor of a Northeast Miami saloon, wants to see certain collateral. If the borrower defaults to a shark, however, the borrower himself knows that the boys are going to put him through a wringer. The basic truth about illegal contracts is that they are unenforceable in the courts. To turn the idea around, the borrower is in no position to claim the protection of the bankruptcy statutes. There are many wild tales about the ways a loan shark collects. In the folklore, the delinquent is visited by a couple of burly young men carrying hockey sticks. In real life, this rarely happens. It doesn't produce money, and the deterrent effect is zero. Anybody willing to pay Shylock interest is already desperate enough not to be deterred by the thought of a beating, unless he belongs to that quirky tribe of people who don't want the money—they want to be beaten for failing to pay back the money. The usury laws are seldom enforced. From a cop's point of view, assault is much better. There the evidence is, in the form of the blood and the broken bones. Eddie would first attempt to foreclose on the collateral, whether it was real property, a relative with an income, a piece of some deal. If worst came to worst, like all lenders who make a mistake, he wrote it off. He couldn't take it as a tax loss because he didn't operate within the income tax system. But he didn't pay taxes on his wins, either.

At this time he had less than $75,000 on the street. And yet he had the usual payments, to cops, politicians, a political law firm. He finished doing his books one evening, on the back of an envelope—again this month his expenses were running ahead of his income—and a man named Lou DeLuca slid onto the stool beside him.

Eddie showed him a big smile. DeLuca gave off a dim glow in return. He had started at about the same time as Eddie. He had either worked harder or connived harder, and he had become a fairly big man in town. He was a specialty accountant, and with all the paperwork these days everybody needs an accountant. He had actually studied for the exam and had the certificate. He was also a gym nut. He worked out four times a week—really worked. Eddie had a hard time trusting any city man in that good shape because you had to ask yourself, what was pushing him to be so perfect?

"Hey, Eddie," DeLuca said lightly, "I've got a friend outside wants to borrow a few bills. Take a ride with us and talk about it."

Eddie said sure. DeLuca drove a new cream-and-tan Continental without a fingerprint on it, a powerful piece of machinery. With DeLuca at the wheel, there was no doubt who was master. No friend was waiting in the car. Eddie knew instantly that this was either a threat or an opportunity. They went up on 95 and out to the Palmetto, merely cruising. DeLuca started by sounding Eddie out about his own situation. The questions showed that he was working from a scouting report and knew Eddie was restless and the regular payments were hurting.

"The thing of it is," Eddie said, wishing he hadn't had two drinks after dinner, "everything's thinned out in the neighborhood. If I have to stay in my old territory, I might as well give up. Even most of the longshoremen have their own houses now, two cars in the family, a mortgage. Good credit risks. So they go to the bank."

And he explained his idea. Loan sharking wasn't a science exactly, but there was more to it than most people realized. What Eddie seemed to be good at was sizing up the prospects of those marginal little businesses that were constantly mushrooming up around town, using mostly Cuban labor, on very small capital. The banks were leery of helping, and the businesses often went under for a want of rainy-day money. But for Eddie to make a loan outside his assigned territory, he had to cut the deal so many ways it was uneconomic. The grease could be awful. A whole lot of that was unnecessary. It had grown up bit by bit over the years. What was needed now was a fresh look at the whole picture.

DeLuca, his eyes sliding between the mirror and the highway, nodded gravely. "It could be I agree with you, Eddie. Where is this fresh look coming from?"

"That's the point."

"It's beginning to seem to me," DeLuca continued, "that a lot of us have been taking the wrong things for granted. We've been drifting, and when you drift, you end up in places you have no business to be. You've been reading those highway articles in the *News*."

Eddie certainly had because there were some major names involved, and he had a feeling that one of the names was going to be mentioned here in a minute. Big

Larry Canada, generally conceded to be top man in illicit gambling when that was where the money was—the mob, they called it then, a word Eddie had never cared for—switched to highway construction at the start of the Interstate program. He had taken a lot of criticism, but his firm had built something like six hundred miles of highway at an average profit of $25,000 a mile. That multiplied out to $15 million in something like five years. You have to book a terrible lot of two dollar bets to get near that figure. In the opinion of DeLuca and a few others, however, not enough of this wealth had filtered back to the people who gave Canada the power base from which he had moved.

"For instance," DeLuca said, "this bind you're in, did it occur to you to take it to Larry and get his advice on it?"

"It occurred to me, Lou, but nowadays—"

"Exactly. He's got more important things, he's busy having dinner with the politicians. I've gone to him time and again, and I've said to him, 'Frankly, you're making a big mistake. Loyalty is a two-way street. You're not just in business to make money. You're a leader, an influence. Sure, it's a new day in a lot of ways, and as far as you personally go, Larry,' I said to him, 'no doubt you've cleaned up. But there are dangers in it. A time may come when you'll wish you stuck more with your friends.' He doesn't thank me for pointing it out."

"Dangers?" Eddie said, picking out that one word, looking away.

"Eddie, do you mind if I give you my ideas? I want to be totally frank."

"God, no, go ahead. I'm interested."

"The way we had it set up before the reorganization," DeLuca said, "and I'm not saying I didn't go along with that and support it, everybody knew where everybody else stood. When something came up, you knew where to go. I don't want to be nostalgic or anything. What the hell, we all had our little angles on the side if it didn't interfere. There was a lot of jockeying always going on, you'll remember that."

"Lou, all I want to do is keep my own nose clean. I stay out of it."

"And that's the smart way to go, believe me," De-Luca assured him. "The more responsibility, the bigger the headache. Larry offered me the job of secretary-treasurer of the road construction, and I turned him down cold. I could see what was coming. My argument with Larry has always been, what good is money if it's just going to end up with the lawyers? This Tim Rourke, the reporter, the way I read those articles, he's hinting he has evidence of larceny and collusion on an enormous scale, and did you see the editorial today calling for empaneling a grand jury? There's already an investigation underway in Tallahassee. More headlines. More bad publicity."

"Right. But I don't see—"

"How it's going to blow back on the rest of us. The highways are more or less a one-man operation, Larry's baby. But he still has the old reputation, Larry Canada, number one guy. He's been called that too many times. Organized crime," DeLuca said with scorn. "I only wish to God it *was* organized. There's no getting around it, a really big stink, with Larry's face on the seven o'clock news every night for six months, will hurt everybody. The cops will stop talking to us till it dies down. What little organization there is now, out the window. And you know Larry. That ego. He'll expect everybody to rally around and contribute. When the sad thing is, nobody but Jumbo and the politicians ever saw any of that ninety percent federal reimbursement."

It was clear by now why Lou DeLuca was looking up a medium-scale Shylock for a private conversation. He wanted to depose Canada before the hurricane struck, and he was lining up support. Eddie didn't commit himself in that first talk because in matters like this there was a heavy penalty for guessing wrong. He decided finally that he couldn't afford not to listen, keeping his options open. Several weeks later, feeling very, very uncertain he was making the right move, he agreed to talk to the other Shylocks on DeLuca's behalf.

He and Canada had once been friends. A couple of times in the early days, Canada would charter a boat to fish off the Keys and ask Eddie along. Eddie could remember every detail of those weekends, who had caught what. They had gone to the jai alai together. That was before Canada initiated a series of tricky maneuvers which ended up with a Canada stooge owning the fronton. They rarely met now. But if Eddie called him and said he had urgent personal business to talk over, Canada would have to see him. He would come alone, and he would arrange for the meeting to take place in some out-of-the-way spot. And Eddie realized, after the third or fourth session with DeLuca, that that was what DeLuca wanted him to do: set Canada up for a hit. Eddie was the ideal person to do it. Without Canada, the highway company would fall apart, the town would get back to normal. Eddie would have a solid in with the new people. DeLuca would go along with whatever he suggested, within reason.

Still, he couldn't decide. The feeling he got as he moved around town was that in a democratic election, with a secret ballot, DeLuca and Canada would break about even. Canada had enemies, but he also had friends. He was tough. He had proved that often enough. He had money to throw around, high-placed friends in both parties, judges. DeLuca, on the other hand, was hungry. There would be less innovation with him. It would be back to nickels and dimes, but the nickels and dimes would be spread among more people. Most of the cops up to the rank of sergeant were for DeLuca; above, for Canada. In a showdown, it could go either way.

DeLuca was pushing him for an answer. Eddie asked for another twelve hours. Moving very carefully indeed, he arranged a meeting with Canada in a restaurant parking lot in Palm Beach and told him what was going on.

Canada had always been a big man—six feet four. He started off heavy, and he had kept adding pounds over the years. Recently, for some reason, he had grown a full beard, making himself one of the most arresting sights in southern Florida. Eddie could see DeLuca's point. Canada was just too visible, an easy symbol for the cartoons. He drove a big Cadillac with a hinged steering wheel that made it easier for him to get in and out, though it was never really easy.

He didn't seem surprised by Eddie's news. "Lou always did have a burr up his ass. I've been expecting something. It's been quiet a long time."

He had brought a package of chocolate chips. He threw a handful into his mouth. He promised to look after Eddie really well if he would keep seeing DeLuca and sneak Canada reports from time to time. To start with, he counted out four five-hundred-dollar bills. Eddie couldn't remember the last time he had handled a five-hundred. DeLuca had given him assurances, but no cash. Eddie felt a surge of his old affection for the big man. At another interview, Canada suggested that for more of those five-hundreds Eddie might be interested in setting DeLuca up when the time came. Maybe, Eddie said doubtfully. If he had a choice, he would prefer to have it done to DeLuca. But bets aren't paid off because the cashier happens to like your looks, only when your horse or dog comes in first. So Eddie continued to hedge. He told DeLuca that Canada must have heard something. Canada had called him in and offered to pay him for information. DeLuca went along with it. And by degrees, Eddie found himself playing the dangerous role of double agent. In books, and probably in life as well, this usually ends badly. Meanwhile he was making money. He was hearing a lot of promises.

But he wasn't getting much sleep, and nothing tasted the way he remembered. Sex had lost much of its edge. He had to work harder to accomplish less. At the most inappropriate moment, he would remember that any day now, any hour, either Canada or DeLuca would call him and tell him the shooters were in town. And he would have to stop wobbling and come down on one side or the other.

Naturally he was watching his step, calling from public phones, looking behind him. He kept getting a prickly feeling. In his hopped-up state, that was a natural reaction, and he nearly decided it was all his imagination. Then he spotted the guy. It was a cop, Jack Downey, who kept what they called the Mafia file and handled the liaison with the FBI and Drug Enforcement. Two times might have been a coincidence. The third time was something to worry about. Eddie did some discreet checking and found that this was all after hours, on Downey's own time. Now what the hell?

Chapter 2

The idea came to Werner French in the middle of the third martini. His second before-dinner drink usually made him gloomy. If he stopped there, he was sure to stay gloomy the whole evening. He always recovered on the third. As he tasted the cold gin poured over fresh ice, he felt that everything would undoubtedly turn out all right. He had a job, a car, a girl. Ninety percent of the population was willing to settle for that. True, it was a terrible job, the car was a rusted-out Chevy. But the girl was first-class—Pam Heller, a spirited blonde who could laugh him out of anything. A marvelous ass, and a mind that jumped like BB's being shaken inside a tin can.

He stood still in the middle of the room. Pam looked at him from the couch. The air-conditioning was laboring tonight, and she was wearing nothing but a one-button blouse.

"I know that look," she said. "You've come up with a solution."

He said slowly, "If we were willing to break the habits of a lifetime—"

"Tell me."

"What you said a minute ago—that the only way I'm going to raise any money is from a loan shark. An electric bulb went on. Something I saw in the *Times*."

The New York Times, Werner believed, was the only newspaper in the country that contained any news, and he read the air-mail edition daily. Putting down his drink, he hunted through the drift of old papers until he found the item. A bookmaker in one of the New York boroughs had been abducted as he left for mass on a Sunday morning. The ransom demand was a modest $150,000. The kidnapped man's family and friends had raised it by suppertime. They just happened to have it lying around.

"One hundred and fifty thousand," Werner repeated, "in the back of the coat closet."

Pam looked up, puzzled. "I don't see it."

"A bookie. You notice they take a light tone. They don't seem to think it was such a dastardly crime. A bookie is already on the wrong side of the law. Anything that happens to him is sort of O.K. *He's fair game*."

"Honey, that's reading a lot into four paragraphs."

"No," Werner insisted. "If he was a lawyer or a storekeeper, they'd be indignant because the hundred and fifty would be real money. But this was a bookie's money, bail money. Not the same thing. Slick and fast. The FBI men don't get called in for twenty-four hours.

Up to that time, it's the local cops. They wouldn't care that much."

"Then let's do it. Do you know any bookies?"

Werner laughed and resumed his pacing. "A loan shark would be better. Cash always on hand. They're unpopular with everybody."

"Do you know any loan sharks? I don't suppose they advertise in the yellow pages."

"You don't think I'm serious. Just because my old man peddles municipal bonds and I have a degree from Columbia School of Architecture, I'm doomed to stay honest. It doesn't follow. I could do it easily."

"Baby, you know you couldn't."

He sat down, no longer laughing. "Well, hell. Cocktail party conversation."

She was totally relaxed, balancing her glass on her stomach. "But we have to do something. I've got that great job answering the phone, and twice a day I'm given the enormous honor of doing a letter for the vice president in charge of young girls. Who gave in to a kinky impulse today and squeezed my breasts because I'd made the tactical error of going to work not wearing a bra—"

"You didn't tell me that."

"One tiny incident among many. It's part of the atmosphere when you work in an office. Every day from somebody. If not a tweak, a look. Why is it all one way? How would he like it if I came up to him and squeezed his cock?"

"He might like it."

"No, he'd fire me. So I quit. I'm going back to New York and take my chances."

Werner said stiffly after a moment, "It's your privilege. We're not married."

Nothing was said for a time. Then Pam stirred.

"Do you mind at all?"

"Damn right I mind. I've tried New York. The building business is so frozen up there—"

"I know," she said more gently. "What I'm edging into, because something is right for you doesn't make it automatically right for me. Things are just—closing in. One year from now, do you want to look back and see three hundred and sixty-five days like today? Or yesterday?"

"We made love a couple of times yesterday, I seem to remember."

"And when it was over, it was over."

He made an effort to get some of the good feeling back. "Will you stay if I kidnap somebody and make a lot of money?"

"Conceivably. How much should we ask?"

Whirling like a gunfighter, he pointed an index finger at the side of her head. "One hundred thousand dollars in hundred-dollar bills, or I'll put a bullet in your ear."

"That's not the way it's done. A note to the wife. One hundred thousand if you want to see your husband alive, and don't tell the fuzz."

"True. For the note we cut words out of the newspaper."

"But not the *Times*. That would give you away."

They did some more improvising, causing the idea to lose what little reality it had had to begin with. But God, if they could pull it off! It was a lovely dream.

Werner had had his degree for two years, and he hadn't set foot in an architectural office. They let him press his nose to the window and watch the draughtsmen, but that was about all. They weren't hiring, they were firing. Firms were merging and shutting down. Housing starts were at their lowest point in thirty years.

And Werner, again in the middle of a third martini, had come up with a great idea. Nobody would pay him to design a house unless he had done a house for somebody else, so they could see how his mind worked. So the thing to do, for Christ's sake, was to borrow money and build a house with himself as client, general contractor, and carpenter. He could sell at cost, below the market, because the object wasn't to make a profit, but to get pictures in the architectural magazines, to become known. He needed $60,000. He went to bankers and got down on his knees. A flat no, everywhere.

"A fantasy," Pam said. "We'll never do anything so adventurous. We might as well fuck. That we know how to do."

Later Werner put on the hamburgers, this being his night to cook. Pam, still in her one-article costume, perched on the counter to watch.

"You know I meant that about New York."

"I had that feeling."

"I have friends there. Here they're all your friends. I'm told I can transfer my unemployment."

"By friends, you mean Les."

She looked at the end of her burning cigarette. "I think he's still there."

"Why shouldn't he still be there? A terrific Brooklyn Heights apartment with a terrace where he can raise his own chives. Expense-account lunches. People ask him to parties—"

She slid off the counter and took him around the waist from behind. "It's so *grubby* here, sweetheart. Let's try being in different places for a while."

He turned the hamburgers. "I thought of somebody who could recommend the right loan shark. That cop, Downey."

Her fingers stopped moving. "You mean bring him in on it?"

"In the planning stage. For instance, how about guns? They're supposed to be so easy to get, but you wouldn't want to use one that was registered in your name. When Downey was here for supper that time, he kept talking about how he hated those people."

"With a passion," she agreed.

"They have contempt for the law. They don't deserve to be protected by the law. Civil liberties for hoodlums? Don't be naïve."

She let go. "But boy, how would you bring something like that *up*?"

"Ask a hypothetical question."

That was all until after dinner. Their eyes met from time to time and jumped apart. Werner really was crazy about this girl. He wasn't sure why. As the songwriters keep saying, the thing is a mystery. She would be a terrible person to go into a kidnapping with, where close timing was essential. She was invariably late. They never got to a movie in time for the titles. He knew she meant it about going to New York. She meant everything she said in that tone of voice. One day in New York and she would be back with Les Carter, the embodiment of everything Werner detested. Bullfight posters on the walls. Wine talk all the time, a subject Les didn't know shit about in Werner's opinion.

Sergeant Jack Downey had come into their life five weeks ago and left it again almost immediately. They came home from a late pizza to find that their house had been thoroughly looted. Luckily Pam had been wearing her good rings. The main thing they lost was the stereo, which dated back to architectural school when Werner was still in his mother's good graces. Sergeant Downey showed up to make them feel better. He had picked up after thousands of these petty break-ins. It happened to everybody, he told them, and there wasn't much you could do. He had hooded gray eyes, heavily creased skin. Whenever he finished one cigar, he lit up another, and they were exceptionally foul-smelling cigars. But Werner, who had sensitive antennae for such things, caught a funny vibration between the policeman and Pam. Among male movie actors, she preferred the veterans, the Charles Bronsons and Robert Mitchums, who had played the same part for decades and acquired a kind of solid strength and authority. Downey's eyes had looked at every kind of depravity, and nothing impressed him anymore. He gave Pam a straight look when he was leaving. The look meant: "If you're serious, fix a time and place and I'll be there."

He dropped in a week later to report the recovery of a truckload of hi-fi components. They didn't include Werner's, and he probably knew that. He probably also knew that Werner worked late Tuesday nights. Werner arrived to find them drinking gin-and-tonics in the kitchen. Downey was telling her some of his career highlights. He had taken his jacket off, and the gun showed. He ended up staying for supper. If he called again, Pam didn't mention it. She made the rules in that area.

In bed, after turning off the light, Werner said abruptly, "In plain English. You're leaving?"

"I really am," she said quietly. They were lying on their backs under the sheet, watching headlights move across the ceiling. "I bought the ticket on the way home. I haven't been brooding about it exactly. It just struck me all at once that I can't live this way."

"It's been nine months. Would you consider rounding out the year?"

"Darling, I can't. That would include my twenty-fourth birthday, and I take birthdays seriously. You don't really want to kidnap anybody, do you?"

"I guess I really don't. The martinis were talking."

"I keep thinking about those people who kidnapped the bookie. They weren't professionals. Professionals would go for higher stakes. They were people like us, Werner! People who needed a specific sum and couldn't get it any other way. They'll never do it again. It took a certain amount of planning, but a hell of a lot less than goes into designing a house. We'd want to research it carefully to be sure of picking the right person. That's why I think Downey's such a marvelous idea. He must have a list of every loan shark in town."

The lifting effect of the gin was completely gone, and the headache was closing in. "How much do you think we'd have to pay him?"

"A full third."

"The whole idea is to keep it small. Finish in twenty-four hours. Pam, seriously—can you see yourself putting a gun in somebody's ribs and telling him to keep quiet and he won't be hurt?"

"Not yet. It makes me sort of shivery. But if you really want some honesty, I feel shivery about New York, too."

"Then don't go, stupid."

"Werner, I have to. Either that or give up."

"We've spent some nice Sunday mornings in this bed."

Her hand gripped his under the sheet. "You know I'm not going to turn into one of those dumb wives."

"Les is pretty bossy with women. You'd have to admire his taste in wines."

"Did I say I'm going back to Les? He was trying to change at the end, but God knows he had a long way to go. I prefer it with you. You know that. But not the way it is now."

"We'd have to rent another house under another name. A different car. Steal one maybe. Think of some clever way to collect the ransom."

"But not too clever. And wear masks."

They were testing each other. Pam was the one who would have to approach Downey. That was the delicate part because of the real possibility that he might pretend to play along, fattening them up for the table—a standard police technique, as they both knew. It would be necessary to feel him out over a number of meetings. Meanwhile she would be postponing her departure, and Werner had a faint hope that even if the thing with Downey didn't work out, she would change her mind about leaving.

They had a spaghetti party. Pam called Downey and told him her friends wouldn't believe she knew a real flesh-and-blood detective, and would he drop in and prove it? Werner had reconciled himself to the fact that they couldn't be sure of Downey—and even then they wouldn't be altogether sure—until Pam had been to bed with him a few times. He didn't like it, but he liked her New York idea even less. He managed to be away the next weekend, looking for work in Tampa. There was as little work in his field in Tampa as there was in Miami. On Monday, Pam reported that Downey had a pragmatic attitude to the matter of under-the-table income. He didn't make regular collections, like many cops. The whole idea of being paid off by those vermin was repugnant to him. He took occasionally, but they didn't pay him. He *took*. He didn't want to co-exist. He wanted to wipe them out. That was his motivation. And in spite of the Nice Nellies and their regulations, he had wiped out a few! He had pulled his twenty-five years, and he could retire any time. But he wanted to make one clean score before he went, to supplement the pension. And loan sharks, it turned out, were high on his list, just below heroin pushers.

Chapter 3

Downey logged a few hundred miles following Eddie Maye and learning his schedule. They decided on a price of $125,000. Eddie wouldn't have that much lying around probably, but he had been part of Larry Canada's organization a long time, and there would be no problem about raising it. Maye lived normally, taking no unusual precautions. He had been picked up several times for one infraction or another, and he had never been caught carrying a gun. Werner liked hearing that. Eddie did things at regular times. He had an easy disposition and never yelled or jumped up and down at the races. Never angry, never in a hurry, he would give them no trouble.

Every Tuesday night, regularly, he visited a woman in Miami Springs. The set-up there was ideal, an attached two-car garage nearly as wide as the house it-self, on a narrow lot. One of the garage doors would be left open for Maye's VW, a weather-beaten red beetle with a joke bumper sticker: "Mafia Staff Car, Keep Ya Mitts Off." Some sense of humor! Eddie followed an unvarying procedure. He drove in, closed the garage door, entered the house through the kitchen, stayed about an hour and a half, and went home. They decided to be in the garage waiting, Werner and Pam—with Downey in reserve in case anything went wrong and they needed a lift getting away. But what could go wrong?

On the Tuesday night they had fixed for the action, Downey was behind Eddie as usual. All of a sudden, the VW turned off abruptly without making a signal, darted into the exit from a shopping-center parking lot, ran through a stop sign on the way out, and was gone by the time Downey recovered. Downey drove straight to the Springs, parked at the curb four spaces down from the woman's house, and waited to see if Eddie would keep his usual Tuesday night date. The garage door was up. The night before, cruising past very late, Downey had shot out the streetlight. In this sort of neighborhood, the sidewalks were never used. He slid low in the seat and started a cigarette.

Inside the garage, Pam and Werner were leaning against the second car, a medium-priced Chevy. They wore loose-fitting sweat shirts and hockey goalkeeper's masks, very spooky, with slitted eyes and savage faces. Werner's long hair, like Pam's, was tucked up in a stocking cap. The props were ready. This was going to be quiet and painless. They had told each other that so often that they nearly believed it.

The TV was running in the house. In the garage, they could hear only an occasional gunshot and the

scream of tires. Werner reached out, and his fingers
grazed an unfamiliar object: she had wrapped strips of
a torn sheet around her chest to alter her silhouette.

"Pretty soon now," he whispered.

"It better be soon."

He followed her arm upward and stopped with his
thumb on the pulse in her throat. It was quicker than
usual. She shook off his hand as a pair of headlights
turned into the driveway.

They ducked out of sight. Werner shook chloroform
onto the pad in his hand. The little car entered the garage, flooding the wall with light. The motor went off,
then the lights.

Werner moved to the front of the Chevy. They had
rehearsed these moves while they were alone. Any
small noises would be covered by the sounds made by
Maye getting out of the car. But Maye held up after
opening the door. Werner's receptors were quivering,
and he heard a slight clicking sound from Pam. Her
teeth had come together.

"Oh, God," Maye said heavily from the VW, "I
don't think I can make it."

He came out. Werner moved, and the garage door
slammed down.

The plan was for Pam to throw the light switch, and
while Eddie was immobilized by the sight of her terri-
fying mask, Werner would come in from behind and
clap the chloroformed cloth over his mouth. But when
the light flashed on, Maye was coming back in the
space between the two cars, and that little change threw
them completely off.

Maye was removing his glasses. He was a plump
man with a ruddy face, usually smiling. Werner knew
Maye had to be scared, but instead of standing

shocked and motionless, permitting himself to be mugged, he went into a flurry of violent motion.

He threw the glasses at Werner and came straight at him, striking him in the face with an extended hand. Werner went backward, and Eddie literally ran right over him. Werner's head made contact with the hard floor. For an instant, things were fuzzy and confused. He managed to roll.

The light went off. A gun banged in the wrong part of the garage. Maye wasn't supposed to be carrying a gun. Downey had practically guaranteed. Maye was at the door now, trying to wrench it open. As Werner came to his knees, his hand closed on something metallic. He had no idea what it was, but it was small enough to throw and he threw it. Another shot from Maye went into one of the cars.

Pam, moving, kicked something over. The garage door went up on its overhead tracks. Werner, suddenly furious at this mild-looking man who ought to be surrendering to them quietly, went over the top of the Volkswagen, leaping on Maye from behind before he could get through the door. He had lost the chloroformed pad. He grappled with Maye, who was trying to bring the gun over his shoulder to shoot Werner loose. They came back hard against the Chevy's fender. Werner shifted his grip. Pam was hitting at Maye's arm with her gun. They would have him in another moment.

Then Downey, in a mask like a skull, stepped in and chopped at Maye's head. The impact was sickening. The taut body went limp in Werner's embrace.

Downey snapped, "Put him in."

In the narrow space between the cars, it wasn't easy. Downey had to do most of it, grunting and swearing.

"We've got about ten more seconds here."

Pam came in the opposite door, and together they wrestled the unconscious loan shark into the narrow space behind the tipped-forward seat. Werner and Downey crammed themselves in. Werner ended up on the driver's side. He fumbled with the switches, and when he had the motor started, he backed out fast. In spite of the shots and the clatter, the neighborhood seemed unchanged.

"Jesus," Downey said with feeling. "Did you fuck that up!"

"He wasn't supposed to have a gun," Werner said.

"You mean it was Eddie doing that shooting? That's funny."

"Funny? I'm laughing."

"Well, we've got the bastard. Take off the masks now."

He stripped off his skull, changing back into Jack Downey, the leathery veteran of twenty-five years in the Miami Police Department.

"So the son of a bitch was carrying a gun. That's going to cost him another twenty-five G's. I didn't even want to be out here, but it's lucky I came. You'd be dead now. If he got out of there, he would have picked you off one at a time."

As a matter of fact, Werner thought they had been doing well without help. The shooting was over by the time Downey got there. But Downey needed to take credit, and that was fine with Werner as long as he was out of their lives at the end of twenty-four hours.

"Stop here," Downey said. "I'll walk back and get my car. If he's too heavy for you, wait for me and I'll help carry him in. Give me about fifteen minutes."

He fixed the dome light so it wouldn't come on when the door opened, got out, and walked away. On the back seat, Maye groaned and flung out an arm.

"We'd better give him the Demerol," Werner said.

Pam rolled back Maye's sleeve. Werner had the loaded hypodermic in a toothbrush box. He tapped Maye's arm smartly with the needle and emptied the syringe. Maye subsided.

"Now we relax and collect the money," Werner said.

They had rented a house in Hialeah, on the other side of Okeechobee Road. Here, too, the garage was attached, but it only had room for one car. There were several "For Sale" signs on the block, and the lawns were baked out and unappealing. Werner was learning that there was no possible way they could foresee everything, and as he got out to open the garage door, a black Labrador frolicked up to pee on the rear wheel.

Werner had trouble making the key work, and before he could get back in the car, the Lab's owner, a middle-aged woman with her hair in curlers, came out of the shadows.

"Alice! Don't do that. You baaaad dog."

The dog leaped on Werner and tried to lick him, glad to find a playmate this late at night. Her mistress scolded her, but so lovingly that she continued to sniff at Werner and slaver on his pants. Werner batted the wet muzzle away.

"Alice, the man doesn't like that. Stop it this minute." The woman pounced and captured the leash. "That's a cute bumper sticker," she said, backing off. "Welcome to Hialeah. I didn't know this place had been rented. It's been empty for weeks."

"Yeah, well," Werner said, trying to conceal how badly the dog had rattled him. "It's a little far out, but one of the nice things, you can keep a dog. That's a Lab, isn't it?"

She said it was, a damn rambunctious one, only a puppy still. Werner said "Well—" again, and backed into the car. Had she noticed the man on the back seat? Maybe, maybe not. He might, of course, be sleeping or drunk.

"Jesus," Werner said when the garage door was down. "What was that crack about a bumper sticker?"

He went behind the car and read: "Mafia Staff Car, Keep Ya Mitts Off."

"She'll remember that," Pam said.

"Now why will she? Nobody's going to hear about this except the people who pay us the money. She won't even know a crime has been committed."

Pam closed with him hard. He felt the gun in her waistband between them and the strange ridges of overlapping cloth under the sweat shirt.

"O.K.," he said, rubbing her shoulder. "Everything's under control."

She whispered, "Werner, let's walk away. It isn't our kind of thing. It can't work for us. Something bad is bound to happen, I feel it."

He pulled back. "Old man Downey wouldn't like that."

"He said there wouldn't be any shooting. He was wrong, wasn't he? I don't trust him. Let's take the car and leave it somewhere. Keep ya mitts off. That's good advice."

He held her so she had to look at him. "You don't mean it."

"I do. I do. Let's get out of this town before we turn into Downey."

"No chance. But if you want to walk out, go ahead and walk. We'll go halves instead of thirds. I'm looking forward to having some money for a change. The hard part is over."

He tipped the Volkswagen seat and began working Maye out. She watched for a moment, then came to help. A dead weight, Maye was hard to manage. They dragged him into the kitchen and on to the back bedroom. There was a mattress here, another in the second bedroom, two folding chairs and a card table in the living room. Maye was breathing harshly, his mouth open. There was a reddish bulge on his forehead where Downey had clubbed him with his gun. Werner tore off a strip of adhesive tape and taped his mouth, then his wrists and ankles.

"He won't feel so hot when he wakes up, but he'll be glad to find out he's still alive. A little poorer, that's all."

When they moved the furniture in, Werner had installed a hasp and staple on the door of this bedroom. He secured it with a padlock.

"Now for a drink," Pam said grimly.

"I still have to drive into town and mail the letter. But save some for me, please. And this may be the time to tell you about a small variation."

They had brought sandwiches and a bottle of scotch. Pam tried to open the bottle, but her fingers were trembling too badly. Werner opened it for her and poured some into a plastic glass. She drank it in two pulls, standing, filled the glass again, and sat down at the folding table.

"What kind of a variation? Jack won't like it unless you cleared it with him."

"Jack is the point, and I didn't clear it with him."

The envelope addressed to Maye's wife was ready to go, but unsealed. Werner was going to post it in the box in front of the main post office, all the way downtown on Fourth Street. It carried a special-handling stamp and would be delivered in the morning. Werner took out the letter and gave it to Pam.

She looked up after a moment. "It says seven o'clock instead of eight."

"Remember the story of the Three Little Pigs? The smart little pig made a date with the wolf to pick apples in the morning, and he showed up an hour early. Jack's a professional wolf. Every now and then, I catch a faint glint. Maybe he thinks he can eat us for breakfast. Maybe he begins to wonder if three-thirds might be a rounder figure than one-third. Haven't you seen some of that?"

"Werner," she said pleadingly, *"why don't we call it off?"*

"That won't be necessary." He took the letter back, refolded it carefully, and licked the envelope. "He has a gun, and we both have guns, but that doesn't make us equal. Neither one of us is a gun person. So we've got to look dumb and stay a step ahead of him. When we sit down at eight to count the money, I want our two-thirds to be somewhere else. That way we have a chance of hanging onto it."

She was staring at him. "I thought for a minute you were going to do him out of his third."

"Too risky. I'm willing to live up to the deal. I just don't want to get screwed."

After a moment, she laughed. "They say a crisis brings out a person's real character. This is a crisis, and maybe this is your true character."

She leaned across, took his face in both hands, gave it a quick shake, and kissed him hard on the mouth.

Chapter 4

Downey came clumping in, throwing off waves of competence and sexual authority. A man who had been around a long time, who wouldn't panic or choke when trouble started. Pam had been bolting her drinks. She was no longer in awe of anybody. Wherever the river took her was where she would go.

Downey jerked his head toward the locked bedroom. "O.K.?"

"Sleeping like an infant," Pam said. "Going up in value every minute."

"Listen, I said tack on another twenty-five," Downey said. "No, that'd be bush. Stick with what we decided, one and a quarter. We know we can get that. Let's see the envelope."

A muscle jerked over Werner's eye, but he gave

Downey the envelope, and Downey checked it for zip code and postage.

"We got a winner here," he said. "Drive careful."

After Werner left, Downey poured himself a drink and reached down to check the shape of Pam's breasts under the sweat shirt.

"Real tits again, that's better. I don't know who you thought you were fooling. You still looked female to me." He looked at his watch. "I want to get laid."

"Yes, sir," she said without moving.

"No kidding. This is the time of night I get my second wind."

"I've noticed."

"Come on. Big event there in the garage. Now I'm going to pay you off." He ran his hand along the edge of her shoulder blade. "You are so damn *thin*. I don't know why I don't end up with cuts all over. Move, will you? We don't have all night."

She fumbled with him for a moment, but she couldn't do it like this. She couldn't switch off one thing and switch on another one second later. His clothes smelled of dirt and sweat and his foul cigars.

"No."

"No?" he repeated.

"Jack, I don't feel like it right now."

"I don't like to stop once I get started. It makes me feel, I don't know, jumpy."

"I don't want to! It's the wrong time, and look at this place. I feel a little sick."

"You'll get over that. You can lie still if you want to, but I'll give five to three I can get you moving."

Pam was revolted by the idea. She tasted whiskey at the back of her throat. Downey took off his pants. He needed a shave, and God, did he need a shower! His hands were filthy. The mattress was ripped and stained. And a lot more was involved than esthetics. She knew it was important not to submit.

"Jack, sit down. We both deserve another drink. Talk about it."

"Fuck that. If you want to talk, talk about it after."

He ate rotten food, fried stuff and cheap hamburgers. He got all his exercise behind the wheel of his car. His ass was too fat. His legs were stumpy.

When he reached for her sweat shirt to pull it off, she said, "You really are a crude monster, Jack. Hasn't anybody ever told you some times are better than others?"

"Too often," he said thickly.

He ripped the sweat shirt over her head, balled it, and threw it across the room. His face changed as the blood flooded into it. The flesh contracted around his eyes. He looked dangerous all at once.

"All right," she said hastily. "But in theory, sex is a two-person thing—the man's not supposed to have fun if the woman's not having any."

"Who said you won't have any?"

He left on his shirt and socks. He was naked in the places where it was important to be naked. She spread her clothes on the mattress and lay down. She knew it would be prudent not to ask Downey to wash. This was one of the most completely unpleasant things that had ever happened to her. He was in less of a hurry now that he had carried his point. He finished his drink, standing.

"That fag," he said, meaning Werner. "He damn near let Eddie get away from him. Somebody who handles money, you can't ever be sure he won't have a gun. But if I'd said there was a chance, Werner would be peeing his pants in there. Be with you in a minute," he added, pouring more scotch.

"Don't feel you have to rush."

A slight breeze was blowing through the open window. Pam was sweating, and the same time she was ice cold. He was a meat-and-potatoes man, Downey. He didn't go in for anything fancy. The first time had been hard, brutal, sudden, and she had responded with a kind of brutality of her own. It had surprised her. Then it had been much less good. He telescoped the preliminaries; he believed he was doing her enough of a favor by being big enough for the entry. It had been a relief to be back with Werner. When Werner liked something, he liked to linger over it. He had real skill and sensitivity. They had reached some astonishing highs. And yet when she dreamed or daydreamed, it was about Downey lately. He had the sureness and strength that Pam lacked and needed.

He came down to the mattress and was soon inside her. His unshaven face ground and scraped against hers. He pounded hard, and at the end she was struggling and gasping.

"Didn't I tell you?" he said, withdrawing.

"Of all the smug bastards—"

Downey grinned. Smug was the word.

"I never had any complaints. If they complain, they know I'll push their face in."

"You big strong complacent men."

"And there's something to be said for experience, too, you know. I've been doing this for quite a number of years."

She would have liked to puncture that conceit by telling him that the reason she had been out of breath was that he had rammed it out of her. She hadn't felt a thing. She stifled the impulse.

He buckled himself into his harness and poured

more scotch. He wasn't quite smiling, but there was something different about him.

"You think I'm a slob, don't you? You and your long-fingernailed boy friend."

"Slob is a bit strong. I was just thinking you remind me of Humphrey Bogart."

"Who?"

"Bogart. He made a million movies. Short legs like you. He looked funny in a bathing suit, but he was very popular in his day."

"I look funny with no clothes on, is that the message?"

She came up on her elbows. "You wanted to get laid. You got laid. Of course you're a bit of a slob, for Christ's sake. That's part of your charm."

"You don't surprise me a bit, you know that? Now I want to take a look at Eddie."

"Don't worry, he's taped up. He's not going anywhere."

"For laughs."

A tag attached to the padlock gave the combination. The unconscious loan shark lay on his side as they had left him, forcing the air in and out through his nose, having bad dreams.

"Eddie, you prick," Downey said with loathing. "Any towels in the bathroom?"

"A couple, why?"

"Bring them."

When she came back, he was fitting a small metal nub to the barrel of his pistol.

"What's that?"

"You ask too many fucking questions."

He folded one of the towels the long way and wound it around Maye's forehead, putting the other folded towel underneath like a pillow. Pam's mind was working slowly after all the scotch. She didn't understand what was happening until Downey picked his gun off the mattress, pointed it at Maye's head, and fired.

It made a snick, not a bang. The body jerked.

Pam seized Downey's shoulder, yelling, "What are you—"

Maye was obviously already dead. His body had arched, and he was lying on his taped wrists. The towel had slipped over his eyes and was already beginning to redden.

"Damn you, you killed him, what did you do that for?"

Downey unscrewed the silencer so he could put his pistol away. She shook his arm and threw it away from her so hard that he had to stagger to keep his balance. She couldn't believe it had happened. Everything was much brighter, in sharper focus, as though the overhead bulb had gone from fifty watts to two hundred.

"Don't worry about it," Downey told her.

"Don't worry about it! Don't worry about it! You killed him!"

She came at him again. He lifted an elbow hard against her breast. The pain cleared her head, and the light in the room returned to normal. She forced herself to look at the dead man, as though hoping he could give her an explanation.

"What are you going to do, bawl?" Downey demanded. "That cock-sucker is a pure Mafia Shylock. Do you know what those people do? If I told you, you'd hold the tears, believe me. They're one hundred percent bad. No redeeming features. Shoot one of them in the head, you're doing a service. Aah—have a drink. We've got to talk before the kid gets back."

Her cheekbones ached, and she could feel needle-points of pain against her eyelids. She covered her face and continued to stand there helplessly until he turned her and forced her out of the room.

"Now I don't want a lot of Goddamn argument. I was going to tell you first, but what's the percentage? You notice I didn't call for a vote. This saves a lot of conversation. It's the only way to get any real money, so for God's sake have a drink and listen."

He pushed her into the chair and splashed scotch into her glass.

"Now drink it, do you want me to pour it in with a funnel? Is that the first stiff you ever saw? You act like it. When you shoot them in the head from six inches they get dead—that's the rule. Think back a half hour. He had a gun, he was trying to kill you. And if I hadn't been there, he would have. And you're crying?"

She tried to say something. All she could manage was, "In cold blood—"

"Cold blood, hot blood, what difference? He's dead, and I'll tell you why I did it if you'll do me the courtesy of listening. Do you think this hasn't crossed my mind dozens of times? You saw one little write-up in a New York paper. Hell, this is happening all over. It's like an epidemic. But you really must be out of your fucking mind if you think I'd take that kind of risk for a piddling forty-one grand."

"The whole idea was that it had to be small."

"That was Wernie-boy's idea, not mine. Look at the stakes here. You stand to lose however many years they decide to give you. I lose that plus my investment in the pension. So I want a big man, and I want big money."

"Who?"

"O.K., now you're asking the right questions. As long as you realize you're not the prosecuting attorney, you're a co-defendant. I didn't pull that trigger all by myself, you helped."

When she started to protest, he said roughly, "That's the law. It's called conspiracy. You brought me the towels. We're all in the kidnapping, we're all in the killing."

"I'm going to be sick."

"No time. Get used to the idea—you can't take the bullet out of his head and put it back in the gun. The cock-sucker's dead, so what do we do now? We move on. I want you to get yourself together so you can explain it to Werner. He's such a daisy, who knows how he'll react? You're tough, kid. You're going to be fine. Because what we're shooting for here is a million bucks, one third of a million apiece. How does it sound?"

She touched the glass to her lips and tossed it back. "Larger." She could feel some of the pounding start to subside.

"That's my little girl," Downey said with satisfaction, sitting down. "It sounds a lot larger. We're going for the top, Big Larry Canada. He's number one on the charts, and if one-twenty-five was right for Eddie Maye, an even million is right for Larry. When you were hinting around about was I open to a proposition, that night you did it with your mouth, I almost busted out laughing. Honey, I've been looking and looking for a couple of birds like you. You're such virgins, nobody would have the least idea. You're going to be out in front, and I'll give odds they'll put me in charge of the investigation. How can we miss?"

"Why did you have to—"

"Stomp on Eddie? Shit, think about it. The bad thing about amateurs is how far can you trust them.

Chapter 5

Timothy Rourke, the Miami *News* investigative reporter, usually worked in the city room, but he had a conference room off it for private conversations and phone calls. Whenever he was working on a major series, he kept his notes there in a locked file. The phone was an outside line so people could call him without giving their names to the switchboard operator. He could also drink there. In the city room, drinking was frowned upon as setting a bad example.

He kept a bottle of Martell's in his desk for his friend Michael Shayne, the private detective. Shayne was with him now. A big, red-haired man who spent as little time as possible in offices, Shayne kept moving, from the conference chair to the window to the corner of the desk. The paper had him on retainer to work with Rourke on the highway story. He was coming off two weeks in Washington, where he had combed the files kept by federal agencies on the Miami criminal infra-structure, looking for anything with a highway connection. Rourke was sorry to be told that he had come across nothing important.

Rourke was thin, gangling, extremely nervous. He smoked continually, to his regret, coughed too much, and had a tendency to miss meals, especially when his work wasn't going well. He and Shayne had teamed up before to pull off some major coups. This time they couldn't seem to make anything start happening. The paper had insisted that he launch the series before he was ready. Sometimes it didn't matter. People would see the headlines and call in with leads. On this one, each day's story was a little more feeble. Duds, they just lay there.

"If you have any good ideas, Mike," Rourke said, "let's hear them. I've had to listen to some heavy sarcasm from upstairs. Am I losing my touch? Possibly. In that case, I may be losing my job. I'm getting high pay with no contract. That means I have to produce."

"They're the ones who insisted on going ahead," Shayne commented.

"That's perfectly true. You tell them. I've tried, but I have a feeling they aren't really listening. They want Canada's head, not excuses."

"What happened while I was getting nowhere in Washington? I could read the clippings, but this way you can leave out the padding."

"That's what it mainly is, padding. One new thing. Pilfering. You have to expect a certain amount of that on every construction site, but naturally on Larry's sites it's organized. There's a hell of a lot of valuable equipment parked out there on the Homestead job, and the guys have been nibbling away. He collects the insurance on it. So far, that's standard. The angle is that it ends up with a crooked used-parts outfit and he buys it back so it can get stolen again. Not that I can prove any of this, but the lawyers say I can use it."

Shayne, a small bubble glass of cognac in his fist, was at the window, watching the traffic. "That won't exactly set the Miami River on fire. Nothing else?"

"Nothing we can print. The tip is that Canada has something going with Phil Gold, the Highway Commissioner. Hell, we all know that. That Palm Beach interchange last year—they changed the location three times, and you know and I know that somebody made a mint. There had to be at least eight million bucks on that platter. Canada and Gold got the major chunks, everybody else got scraps. But the lawyers say it's actionable unless we can trace the real estate transfers, and the boys did a marvelous job there. It's like a stream of water coming into a desert. It disappears. We'd need subpoena power and a blanket promise of immunity. That means a grand jury. We can't get a grand jury unless we come up with something major. So there we are."

"We don't need documents. A clandestine meeting between Canada and Gold would do it."

"Sure. The crook and the Highway Commissioner. Why would they be getting together except to work out a deal? That's why I wanted you back early. I have a feeling something's about to break."

Shayne sat down. "Trying to follow Canada would be a waste of time, Tim. He's too good at the game. I explained this all to your editorial board. I'd need three cars with two-way radios, and that kind of operation is hard to hide. He wouldn't do anything but go out to eat and play golf."

"The paper wouldn't pay for three cars, anyway. They want the story, but they don't want it to cost them anything extra. So I put Frieda on the opposite end, the Gold end. There's so much security on those state jobs that they get careless sometimes. She has a Tallahassee agency working twenty-four hours. I don't think they're likely to lose him."

"Twenty-four-hour coverage. That's expensive."

"Well, it just struck me." He waved at the scribbled notes and clippings spread across the desk. "Every one of the ways Canada scoops in the dough—the insurance deal, the consultant fees that go into the cost base, the kickbacks from subcontractors, all the skimping on specs, the patronage no-show jobs—he can't exploit any of that unless he gets the contract in the first place."

"You startle me, Tim," Shayne said dryly.

"All right, it's obvious, but how do they make sure he's always the low bidder? They're sealed bids. Companies from all over come in to bid on those jobs. Granted, the real money comes from the angles he works later, but everybody else knows those angles as well as he does. There are fortunes to be made in highway construction, and some of those guys would put in negative bids to get a shot at the skim. But since Gold has been commissioner, Canada hasn't lost a competition. That's an interesting streak."

"You can print that."

"But I can't draw any conclusions, the lawyers tell me, without some hard evidence of collusion. All right. The Everglades link-up. Seventy-five comes down the Gulf Coast, 95 down our side, and the highway freaks can't relax until they get them connected. We have two days before Gold opens the bids. Canada will be bidding as usual. There has to be some kind of communi-

cation before then, and would they do it by telephone?
I doubt it. If we can't catch them at it, I'll have to
advise the paper to close down the series."

The phone rang. Rourke picked it up and listened.
"Shayne? Yeah, he's here, but if he's already said
no—"

He listened another moment, and Shayne saw his attention sharpen. "I'll check." He covered the mouth-
piece. "It's a woman named Chris Maye. Her husband
got killed last week."

"I talked to her," Shayne said. "Not a hell of a lot I
could do even if I had time. Look for a snitch, and the
cops are better at that than I am."

"She says he was kidnapped, and he was a Canada
man. What do you think? Let's listen to her."

Shayne shrugged. Rourke told the woman he would
send a copy boy out to show her the way. He went to
the door and yelled.

"The radar is working," he said, coming back.
"Blip, blip, blip. Something is going on in this town."

"Something generally is."

"No," Rourke insisted, coughing. "It's like that five
minutes before a hurricane. You know something's different. This highway series—why haven't people been
calling me? We've had one good tip, just one, the
Gold–Canada tie-up. I know it's authentic, but the guy
who gave it to me didn't owe me that big a favor. He
owed me a favor, but more on the order of a super-
fecta at Pompano. Who stands to benefit? If Larry
Canada is cut up and thrown to the sharks, who inher-
its? It strikes me that I don't really know."

"You're the number one crime reporter in Miami. If
you don't know, who does?"

"Hell, all the number one crime reporter knows is
what people are willing to tell him, and lately some of

my friends have been crossing the street when they see me coming. Mike, the thought hit me when this woman was talking. What if that wasn't a real kidnapping? What if it was only a cover to knock over a Canada man without starting a war? When that kind of high-level argument is going on, there are ways you can milk it. Or you can end up in the middle," Rourke added, "which has happened to me a few times, as I know you remember, so I'm walking short. Nothing impulsive and sudden, like the old days." He tapped his forehead. "I'm going to think before I jump."

Shayne laughed. "I'll believe that when I see it."

Shayne had long experience with Rourke's extrasensory hunches. They bit him hard, and while he was feeling their effect, he wasn't open to rational argument. Still, once in a while they paid off, and Shayne had learned not to disregard them completely. Several winters before, with Shayne scoffing most of the way, one of these hunches had carried Rourke into an investigation that led to a Pulitzer prize.

The copy boy came in with a nicely dressed woman wearing glasses, who introduced herself as Chris Maye. In Eddie Maye's world, the wives seldom get taken to the races or the games, and Shayne was meeting her for the first time. She refused Rourke's offer of a drink, but accepted a cigarette. When that was out of the way, she said abruptly, "I have twenty-five thousand dollars. I don't know what you usually charge, Mr. Shayne, but I don't know who else I can go to. I haven't slept more than an hour at a time since Eddie—"

The rest of her breath came out in a sob. Rourke was around the desk in an instant. He was surprisingly good with grief-stricken women. He patted her, gave her Kleenex, poured whiskey, and made her drink it. Shayne let him handle it. He had liked her husband, but there was nothing surprising about his early death. Loan sharks have only a slightly longer life expectancy than racing-car drivers.

Ater a time, Rourke said gently, "Can we talk about it, Chris?"

"We have to talk about it." She blew her nose hard. "I'm not a weeper and a wailer as a rule. I want to find out what happened to Eddie so it will have some—meaning. Or shape. I don't know how to say it."

"How much did you use on it, Tim?" Shayne said.

"Couple of paragraphs. Found slain, was about all. Chris, will it bother you if I tell him?"

"In a phone booth outside the Bowl," she said, looking down at the wadded Kleenex. "A bullet hole in the head. There wasn't much—mess, considering. He had tape marks on his mouth and wrists. The phone booth was where I was supposed to leave the money."

"Do you have a ransom note?"

She took out a folded paper, on which the instructions and the usual threats were printed in ragged capitals.

"'He will be killed,'" she said, quoting. "'You will never see him again unless instructions are followed, to the letter.' So I followed instructions, to the letter. The strange thing is that I wasn't especially scared. It sounded so businesslike, it didn't occur to me that if I met their price they wouldn't deliver. I scurried around, saw a few people—"

"Can we stop there?" Rourke said. "Did these people include Larry Canada?"

"Of course. You know how Eddie made a living. He didn't keep it a secret. But he wasn't part of any God-father organization or anything like that. He used to laugh about the stories in the papers. I know you have to simplify things, Mr. Rourke, use labels and so on.

'Alleged,' 'reputed,' 'according to law enforcement officials—' Most of the law enforcement officials I've ever run into are morons. Eddie and Larry grew up in the same neighborhood, that's all it amounts to. Larry took bets, Eddie made loans. I needed a hundred thousand to go with this twenty-five. Larry collected it for me. I don't know how Eddie would have paid him back, but he's been talking about selling the business."

"It says seven o'clock," Shayne said. "Were you on time?"

"Exactly on time. There was an out-of-order sign on the phone. Eddie was scrunched down on the floor with another note in his mouth."

She took out another printed message, in the same green ink as the ransom note. This one had been rolled instead of folded. It said: "SORRY. EDDIE TRIED TO SAVE YOU SOME MONEY. HE'LL KNOW BETTER THE NEXT TIME."

"Eddie," she said, "my God, I've been married to him eighteen years. He wasn't one of those show-off masculine types. He went along. He rolled with the punches. There were other things in his life besides money. He would have done what they told him, and made a funny story out of it when he came back."

She had been doing well after a difficult beginning, but now she tightened up and began crying again. "We never had children. We were still trying. Eddie was so good with his nephews and nieces, the kids on our street. Something like a car crash, an accident, I could have adjusted to that. But if it's some kind of political thing—"

They were watching her closely. She explained, "Not that kind of politics. To get control of those businesses, the gambling and all."

"That's what my blips have been telling me," Rourke said with a glance at Shayne. "And if you can give us some more on that, maybe Mike will reconsider and say yes."

She shook her head helplessly. "I'd wake up in the middle of the night and feel him lying there with his eyes open, stiff as a board. All he ever said was that he was trying to make up his mind which way to jump. He thought I was better off not knowing about it. I keep puzzling about things. What happened to his car? Why hasn't it turned up? He was collecting money that day. He had a lot of cash. I saw it—a lot. What happened to it? And if this was an ordinary kidnapping, wouldn't they try to collect and then throw the body in a canal? Isn't that what you'd do?"

"That's been standard since the Lindbergh baby," Rourke said. "Have you told the cops any of this?"

"Certainly not. And I don't intend to. I took the note out of his mouth and let somebody else find him. When they called me, I went down and identified him. Eddie Maye, reputed or alleged or reported to be a notorious loan shark, killed by one of his business rivals or by a customer he squeezed too hard. The police in this town don't solve any of those. One criminal less is the way they look at it. Well, Mr. Shayne?"

She took three packages of bills out of her purse and put them on the desk, squaring them neatly. "This was in Eddie's safe-deposit box. If it isn't enough—"

"It's too much," Shayne said. "Put it away. I can't take it. There's a rule against working for two clients at the same time. Tim's paper is paying me full rates, and they expect my full attention. But what you've been telling us is very interesting. Canada has been refusing to see us, and this gives us a lever."

The phone rang, and Rourke dived at it.

"Frieda, Mike."

Frieda Field ran her own detective agency, Field

Associates, with an office in Miami Beach and retainers from several of the Beach hotels. The agency had belonged to her husband, who had been killed a few years before. She had elected to continue the business and had turned out to be good at it. Rourke had brought her in to keep track of the comings and goings of Philip J. Gold, the State Highway Commissioner, who might or might not have concealed dealings with Larry Canada, their principal target. Frieda was a handsome woman, dark-haired, slender, with a beautifully coordinated body, and yet to someone worrying about being followed, she was all but invisible. How could such a great-looking woman have the humdrum job of finding out if a certain state official was meeting the president of a certain road construction firm?

"I'm at a gas station off Route 10, Mike," she said, "and I think he's gassing up for the Interstate. He's getting a sandwich, and it's the wrong time for food unless he plans to skip supper."

Shayne checked his watch. It was five-fifteen.

"Anybody with you?"

"No. But I've got the van, and I'm dressed as a tourist. The bike on the rack—everything. I won't be noticed as long as he stays on the highway. I'll need help if he goes all the way. Here he comes now."

Shayne quickly told her he would check with the mobile operator and pick her up above Palm Beach.

"To wind up what I was saying," he said to Mrs. Maye, after hanging up, "I didn't take this job with Tim because of the money they're paying me—"

"Which is lucky," Rourke said, "because they're not paying him a hell of a lot."

"And I don't think many problems will be solved by putting Larry Canada in jail. People are standing in line to take his place. But I've spent a lot of time out in the Glades, and I hate to think what that highway could do to it. With a little luck, we may be able to stop this one. Before you came in, I was trying to tell Tim how I felt about Eddie. I've known legitimate bankers I've liked less. I'm sorry he's dead, and killing is the one crime I can still get worked up about. Tim tells me we have a forty-eight-hour deadline, and I hope he can think of things to keep me busy. I'll call you at the end of the week and let you know how it's going. Meanwhile I think you ought to take it to the cops."

She shook her head again and said quietly, "That would be the wrong thing, Mr. Shayne. The night before it happened, we were having one of those rigid periods around two o'clock, and Eddie suddenly got up and went to the window and said he was being followed by somebody. Everywhere. He was really worried about it. A cop. He didn't tell me the name."

Chapter 6

Werner French hesitated before getting out of the car and going in the house. Always a little too stiff and serious, he looked mad all the time now, with a sullen, rebellious set to his mouth. He would try to clean everything out of his mind and relax. Sometimes he was able to manage it for a minute or two, and then he would be up and walking, hammering his bunched fingertips against the side of his leg.

Pam came out of the bedroom to greet him. She had been extremely sweet since the catastrophe with Eddie Maye, he had to admit. She fucked like an angel, with none of her old brusqueness and asperity. And this had the odd effect of making Werner more aware of her faults. He had thought up this crazy kidnapping scheme to keep her from running off to New York. It had failed, it had failed fairly spectacularly, but even if the damn thing had worked, would it have been worth it? It would have knotted them together for the foreseeable future. And he could do without that excitement, the constant state of crisis, the mood swings, the ups and downs. He wanted some peace.

She came against him hard. "Baby, I can't bear it when you're gone that long. You used to be so predictable. Where have you been?"

As a matter of fact, Werner had been nowhere in particular, doing nothing furtive or dramatic. Feeling restless and impatient, he had wanted to drive around, just get in the car and drive the expressways, but he was terribly low on cash, and gas costs money these days, they no longer give it away free. So he had walked around the big downtown marina and looked at the big, brutal, expensive boats. Boats are less regimented than cars. They don't need to stay on the highways. On a boat, you can go anywhere in the world that recognizes an American passport, and of course most places do.

"Killing time was all," he said, moving away. "Thinking."

"Don't think!" she said sharply. "Drift. That's the only way to get through this. And Werner," she added as he opened the bottle, "maybe we ought to stick to coffee? A clear head would be a good idea if we have to do any fast driving. Jack may be calling any minute."

"A lot of minutes have gone by lately, waiting for Jack."

"Everything has to be just right. I want to get it over with, too, but if hurrying means taking chances— Baby, come to bed. I want to."

Werner smiled, drinking. "We've been getting a lot of that, haven't we?"

Actually, from the moment they loaded the dead body of Eddie Maye into the back seat of his VW and Downey drove off, their lovemaking had been practically continuous. They had gone back in the house and made love without even washing the traces of Eddie off their hands. It was astonishing to Werner that such a thing could happen, but it definitely did happen. And after returning to their own house, they continued to sleep and make love almost around the clock. If they ended up in separate cells, they would have much to remember. They crammed an ordinary month's episodes into five days. And it cured Werner, cured him for good. He entered her body with increasing reluctance. She had been getting wilder and wilder at the end, throwing herself around, making strange tortured sounds, and sometimes, as happened now, bursting into tears.

"Werner, if I'd only remembered that damn padlock—"

He stroked her mechanically. "If-only is a dumb game. If Jack had only noticed. If we'd put a couple more cc's of Demerol in that jolt. And incidentally, let's make sure of that this time. Canada's a big fat man. Give him a double."

"But we can't make it too strong or we'll kill him."

Werner reached for his drink. "I haven't asked you this yet, but it's been on my mind. How did Jack do it? Did he just walk over and shoot, or did he have to talk himself into it?"

"It seemed to be easy for him. You have to remember—a loan shark is like a coyote to Jack. You don't kill it, you harvest it to keep down the population."

"You didn't try to argue him out of it?"

"Are you crazy? It happened so fast, I was badly in

shock. The minute he did it, you could see that Nean-
derthal brain starting to tick. The coyote was dead.
Was there any way we could use it?"

"If you want to know my opinion, I think he had
that in mind all along. He was just waiting for an opening. Like this, he could shift some of the blame to you,
make you feel guilty."

She was silent for a moment. "I've thought of that.
We can't have more sex right this minute, and it
wouldn't be smart to get drunk, which ordinarily I
wouldn't mind doing, so I suppose we'll have to talk
about it. Here's what I decided. I decided that whether
he did or didn't, it doesn't matter. We did the kidnapping together. We're all in the same boat now."

"Not quite in the same boat," Werner said. They
never looked directly at each other when they were
talking about anything serious, as though afraid of
what they would discover. "There's one big difference.
He's a cop. We're nobodies. If anything slips, he can
bust us, or shoot us in the head the way he did Eddie,
then arrange it any way he likes. And keep all the
money."

After another moment, she said in a low voice, "It
might be better for our mental health if we didn't wonder about things like that."

"How much money have you got?"

"Scraping bottom. You?"

"Enough for groceries for another week. You can't
hide from a mad cop on unemployment insurance. So
maybe we have to go through with this."

"Except that"—she waited—"it might be a good idea to
keep in mind what you're saying about Downey after
we collect the money—"

"I'm for that," he said briefly.

She reached for cigarettes. She had lost weight. She

was so close to the tipping point that unless she made a conscious effort to eat, it showed almost at once. She had too many knobs on her spine, and a starved ass. Incredibly, because it had been less than five minutes, he felt the beginnings of the sexual tingle. But the phone rang.

The phone table was on Pam's side of the bed. Her shoulder muscles knotted. He could tell it was Downey, and the time had come.

"All right. Yes, twenty minutes. Yes. Don't worry about that. We're all psyched up." Putting the phone down, she said, "Get dressed."

They met at a drive-in movie. It was porno night, two of the new generation of porno pictures, with a grammatical script and personable actors who gave every appearance of enjoying what they were doing. Interesting, complicated things kept taking place on the oversized screen, and when Downey's car appeared at the lighted ticket window, Werner almost missed it. They waited to be sure nobody had followed him in, then threaded their way among the darkened cars with the entwined couples and got in with him. This was his working vehicle, with metal mesh separating the front and back seats and no inside handles on the rear doors. They had already had one conference in this car, and it made Werner uncomfortable, reminding him forcibly of one of the things that could very well happen.

"The Goddamn perverts," Downey snarled, looking up at the screen. "Showing this dirty stuff, and not a thing in the world we can do about it. We can't lay a finger on them. The Supreme Court said so. I'll tell you one thing," he said, turning, "people are fucking in these cars."

"Maybe we can find a John Wayne movie the next time," Werner said.

"You realize people can see that screen from the expressway? By Christ, I'm going to come in here some dark night with a chain saw—"

Werner felt the back of Pam's hand pressed warningly against his leg. He decided there was no point in quarreling. Downey wasn't too bright, but they were stuck with him.

She said, "We didn't come here to talk about free expression on the screen, did we, Jack? Call the meeting to order."

Downey swung all the way around. He had left the sound outlet hooked to the post. On the screen behind him, three lovely young women continued to work in silence.

"It's tonight," he announced. "And we couldn't ask for a better location. Man, it couldn't be more ideal. This is going to be so easy."

"Not like the last time," Werner couldn't help saying.

"Wernie," Downey said after a slight pause, "could something be bugging you? Let's talk about it."

Werner moved his hand so it gripped Pam's. Her fingers lay inert in his to show that she didn't think this conversation was necessary.

"As far as Eddie Maye goes," Werner said, "I guess you were right. We seem to be in the clear. A three-inch story in the paper, and nothing else. One more unsolved homicide for the end-of-the-year stats."

"And it's going to stay unsolved all the way," Downey said. "My partner on it is a real retard. All he likes is to drink beer and watch games on TV. An unsolved *gangland* homicide, Werner. We don't care if they only kill each other."

"I accept that, and I know you can jinx a thing if you get too negative about it. But let's suppose for a minute. What if some little unexpected thing goes wrong, like that gun Eddie had when he was supposed to be so meek and mild. Knock on wood. I mean, *what if*? Won't they ask themselves, even your partner if he can tear himself away from the tube for a minute, whether we're the same people who did it to Eddie? And that's so very much more heavy."

Somewhat to Werner's surprise, Downey didn't start yelling. "I'm glad you brought this up, Werner," he said seriously. "Remember—we don't officially know that was a kidnapping for ransom. Speaking as a cop now. But there's always that outside chance that the two things would be connected. As far as I'm concerned, it's a plus. I don't want to insult you or anything, but this is your first time at bat in the majors. If it comes down to where you have to shoot the mother or somebody else, now I can count on you to perform. You won't check or hold back. Because it's your ass, right? And one of the things I was starting to tell you, it looks so open and shut I'm going to be right there with you on it."

"I'm glad to hear that," Pam said.

"When you got in that trouble in the garage," Downey continued, "I could have turned my back and let you get out of it by your own self. Wading into the middle of a gunfight wasn't a part of my deal. But it didn't occur to me not to. When Pam goofed at the house and let Eddie see us, I'm the one who took care of it, didn't I? We're getting a fantastic break tonight. Unbelievable. And if you're a believer in luck, Werner—we all are—you can't walk away from a break like that, or the luck will be rotten the rest of your life, and you'll die young. O.K.? O.K., Pam?"

"O.K. But can we get going, please? All that stuff up there is making it hard to concentrate."

Downey shot a quick glance over his shoulder. "Say a carload of nuns came driving along and saw that? Do you see what I mean? Consenting adults is one thing—"

"Jack."

He turned back. "Just don't look, or cover your eyes. The big thing I've been trying to do is get a bug in on Canada. But he's bug-shy from way back, and he's got some advanced sweeping equipment. When he goes places, he goes with a driver mostly. And he don't keep to a schedule, a pattern, you know? He learned that a long time ago. So I had what I think was an intelligent idea for a change. He's got a piece of business coming up with Phil Gold, the Highway Commissioner, I happen to know, and they're going to have to get together. So I took time off and went up to Tallahassee and tapped in on Gold's personal phone. I've been flying up every day to listen to the tapes, and today we hit oil. Canada. He didn't give his name, but I know the bastard's voice. Started off with a certain amount of this-and-that about politics for camouflage. Then he said he was going to be at the hot plant tonight at around eleven. The hot plant. Does that ring any bell with you? It didn't with me at first, either, and then all of a sudden I got it. That's what they call the asphalt thing on a construction site. The big machine that mixes up the asphalt. Now at eleven at night, naturally it wouldn't be working. But if anybody saw one of their cars, it wouldn't be out of line. The Highway Commissioner, he could be pulling an inspection. Canada owns the company, he has a perfect right to be there."

"Where?" Werner said.

"That big Homestead interchange, two four-lanes coming in and crossing, with the cloverleafs. So what I did, I got in the department chopper and told the guy to drop me down on Homestead Air Base. Chasing a lead on Eddie Maye was the idea. And I had a chance to study the site from four hundred feet. It's perfect all around. Perfect for Canada to meet somebody, and perfect for us to grab him."

He was trying to stay cool, but he had trouble keeping the excitement out of his voice. "I'm going out on a limb and predict that Larry's going to be driving himself, no driver. Never mind if he brings somebody, we can handle it. But from the way they talked on the phone, this is really under the table. He'll make damn sure nobody's behind him, but that won't apply to us because we'll be there already. There's a side road three-quarters of a mile away where we can leave the car. A chain-link fence to get through, but that's no problem. I've got a good pair of bolt-cutters."

"A night watchman?" Werner asked.

"Now you're using your head," Downey said approvingly. "Sure, but if Canada set this up for a hundred percent privacy, won't he tell the guy to go into town and buy himself a few beers? He's the big boss, he can do how he pleases. We'll ease in very slow. If anybody's there, I know you'll be willing to let me handle it."

"More than willing," Pam said.

"And would I be getting this involved if I didn't think it was sure-fire? It's made to order. These dozens of big machines, plenty of places of concealment. If they do what I want them to, they'll come in separately from opposite directions. If they're going to be looking at maps or specs, they'll go in one of the trailers. They shouldn't be having this conversation so they're going to be easy to spook. Say while they're inside, we do something to Canada's car, cut the ignition cable. Are you picturing this? Gold is appointed. The Governor can cut off that appointment on ten seconds' notice. So he'll be carrying a very strong charge. At the first sign of trouble, he'll be out in his car so fucking fast. And Canada will feel awful lonely. No driver, no watchman."

"No gun?" Werner said.

"Did I say that? Larry Canada wouldn't want to be picked up on a gun violation, but tonight could be the exception. Three guns to one. What somebody like Canada does when he's outnumbered, nine times out of ten, he surrenders. They talk tough, but they have the balls of a rabbit. We don't have to move in on him until he gets in the car. He's a big heavy man. He has to cramp himself in and out. No, hang on, even better. Werner—that's a big four-door, a Caddy. You can be down out of sight in the back seat. You'll know when he gets in because that car is going to shake and settle down on the shocks. Rear up with the chloroform. The steering column will be pinning him in."

"We'll move him in his car?" Pam said.

"Have to. Give it a jump start. With a gun at the back of his head, he'll remember what happened to Eddie Maye. Larry's rough-housing days are long in the past, but let's not take chances trying to get him to change cars under his own power. I don't want to have to shoot this one. Give him the shot right away and manhandle him. How does it sound?"

He wanted approval, and Werner said grudgingly, "Frankly, I can't see anything wrong with it."

"Wrong with it, it's sensational," Pam said. "I can smell money from here."

Downey nodded. "Then let's get the hell out there and set up."

Chapter 7

Gold, in his state car, came south on Interstate 75. He was over the limit, and at one point a highway patrolman chased him for a short way before noticing the low-number official marker. Frieda Field, behind him, had driven this highway frequently. Most of the time, she hung far enough back to keep her lights out of his mirror, closing with him only as he was approaching an exit. When he committed himself to the turnpike, she knew he was going all the way. She picked up the Orlando mobile operator and had her put through a call to Shayne.

Shayne met them at Palm Beach. He was parked at the foot of the West Palm ramp, hunched over the wheel, rearranging the pieces of the story they had been told by Chris Maye. He was trying to see some

connection between her dead husband, Eddie, the
small-time loan shark, and Larry Canada's multi-
million-dollar highway deals. They were on different
levels, like the intersecting traffic here. The woman
herself interested him. It had seemed to Shayne, listening quietly, that there was something she was holding
back.

Frieda's van sailed serenely past. It was a big Dodge
Sportsman, somewhat top-heavy on secondary roads,
but powered with a Mercedes engine, capable of staying with all but the hottest cars on the Interstate. Her
headlights flicked, and Shayne moved smoothly into
the entry lane. It was ten-thirty. There was still considerable traffic.

The Miami mobile operator connected the two cars
and then backed out of the conversation.

"He may be running a bit late," Frieda said. "It's a
dark blue Chrysler, a seal on the door and state plates.
How do we proceed?"

"You stay back and I'll pass him. Watch for me at
Lake Worth. How are you, Freida?"

"Glad to hear a friendly voice. He's a dull man, and
I've been having a dull time."

"There's a deadline coming up, and we may be
seeing some action. He drove down instead of flying.
That may mean he's meeting somebody he's not supposed to know, like Larry Canada."

"And wouldn't that be nice?"

"We haven't developed much at our end. Tim's in
one of his gloomy moods. Sometimes that's when
things begin to happen."

"About time, in my opinion."

Shayne pulled out to pass. The van clearly belonged
to a vacationer, not a private detective. A bicycle was
strapped to the back door. The bumpers were plastered

with ads for various tourist traps between Miami and
Chicago. She was using Illinois plates. Coming abreast,
he held steady for a moment. Frieda was wearing a
brief halter and a long-billed fisherman's cap. She gave
him a mocking salute, which he returned with a smile.

He zoomed past.

He ran up swiftly on the blue Chrysler. As he went
past, he had a sideward glimpse of a gray-haired man,
clean-shaven, wearing a bureaucrat's steel-rimmed
glasses and a look of generalized anxiety. He was grip-
ping the wheel hard, and Shayne had the impression
that he was going faster than he would usually think
was safe.

At the next exit, Shayne dropped off, paid the small
toll, and waited for the appearance of the Chrysler. It
passed without slackening speed. The mobile operator
had his connection ready, and Shayne told Frieda that
their man was still on the highway. He picked up a
new ticket and rejoined the pursuit. It was a system
they had used before, and as long as the phones stayed
open, it was almost impossible for even the most experienced dodger to lose them.

They continued south. The Chrysler followed arrows
into the long bypass around Miami. This was newly
laid highway, and most of the traffic dropped off at the
Miami exits. Now the van, with the pretty young
woman at the wheel, became more conspicuous. Gold
began driving more slowly, perhaps pacing himself to
arrive somewhere at a percise moment. Shayne waited
to pass until he was partially screened by a truck, then
sped ahead to the next-to-the-last exit. This was construction country, with occasional one-way stretches,
long lines of flaring smoke pots and blinkers.

He was watching for the Chrysler, and saw the van
first. He signaled for Frieda to pull over.

"The big construction five miles back," Shayne said. "That has to be it. Let's go back and take a look."

The median strip, a wide buffer separating north-bound and southbound traffic, had just been planted with grass. Signs warned them to keep off the shoulders, as there weren't any, and they continued south to the next truck crossing, made the U-turn, and headed back toward the smoke-pot fires through an unfriendly environment that might have been blasted by B-52's. A succession of increasingly urgent warnings alerted northbound cars to be prepared to shift into a one-way pattern that would continue for the next eight miles. It was a bottle neck during the day, but less serious at this time of night. Shayne pulled up as the turnoff approached.

"It's passable," he said when the van stopped alongside. "The Highway Commissioner doesn't have to pay attention to his own signs. But we'd better walk in. They'll be watching for headlights."

Getting out, he moved some of the flaring pots so they could drive through. They parked the vehicles out of sight of the highway. Before leaving the car, Shayne pressed a recessed spring in the door panel and a Smith and Wesson .367 dropped into his hand.

"It's going to be like that, do you think?" Frieda said.

"There's a huge amount of money involved."

The gun went inside his shirt. He unlocked the trunk and from a well-organized built-in cabinet took a tiny camera and a pair of night-vision binoculars.

"Let's use the bicycle," Frieda said. "We don't want them to be gone by the time we get there."

"I haven't ridden a bike in years."

"That's one of the things you only need to learn once."

Unstrapping the bike from the rear of the van, she trundled it out on the smooth pavement while Shayne lined up the pots again to discourage other cars. He straddled the bike, an English ten-speed. Frieda perched on the center bar, where she blocked access to the shifting levers. Starting in one of the middle gears, they wobbled away, beginning to run true as they gathered speed.

Frieda gave a low laugh. "Mike, this is funny."

"Is it?" he said, pedaling grimly.

The set of the handlebars invited him to crouch forward, but of course Frieda was in the way. A slight downward incline helped a little, and then their momentum carried them up one of the barely perceptible rises that are southern Florida's equivalent of hills. He caught the rhythm and soon was pedaling more strongly. It was a black night, without stars or moon. The lighter-colored sand on the shoulders kept him on the asphalt. The median was wider here, twenty yards or so of broken ground strewn with construction litter. On the far strip, orange barrels and an occasional flare reminded drivers to stay in their own lanes. Free-standing concrete pillars loomed ahead like a roofless temple. Creeping out at right angles was the new highway, which in a few years' time would allow wheeled traffic to reach Card Sound and the bay. There was nothing much there now except sand and scrub. The highway people urged skeptics to think back to the 1920's. When the Florida East Coast Railway started south from Palm Beach, Miami was only a village, little larger than Homestead today. People would follow the highway.

Shayne came back on the pedals, forgetting that the brakes were on the handlebars. By the time he found them, he and Frieda were off in the sand.

Frieda extricated herself. "Going back," she whispered, "I'll pedal."

An immense culvert was being installed here to carry an irrigation canal, which had to cross the new highway. Great lengths of pipe blocked access to the other strip. A paving machine, waiting for daylight, dominated the smaller vehicles grouped around it. Shayne left the bike in its blacker shadow, climbed up carefully under the big umbrella, and broke out the binoculars.

The truck park, with long ranks of earth-moving and paving equipment, lay in a shallow, dishlike depression to the right, in what would eventually be the armpit of the intersection. There were a half-dozen light poles carrying the spread wings of mercury-vapor lights, but these had been turned off so the surreptitious meeting could take place in darkness. He adjusted the focusing knob and began looking for private cars. Everything had a queer reddish tone, as though seen through a filter.

After one quick sweep, he began to see some order in the apparent chaos. A dirt road, passing out through a chain-link fence, must lead to the new construction, the broad sandy gash that was being driven from Homestead to the bay. That road and four others became the spokes of a great wheel. At the hub sat the huge mixer—a semipermanent installation where the oil, sand, and gravel came together to be cooked. Two of the spokes ran outward to low banks of sand and gravel, which had been eaten at by payloaders. From huge bins on either side of the mixer, sand and gravel spilled onto conveyor belts leading to the apertures in the face-plate of the great revolving tank. Mixed and heated, loads of the hot goo would be drawn off into trucks and carried out to the pavers. The mixer itself was controlled from a command trailer, tied to the feeds and motors with a variety of umbilical connections.

Headlights gleamed in the distance, traveling south. Magnified by the magic of his night glasses, the splinter of light permitted Shayne to pick out the shape of a parked car between the control trailer and a blocked-up tanker the size of a beached whale. He held the glasses steady. The next headlight gave the car dimensions and character. It was long and stately, with the distinctive grill and regal rear end of a Cadillac.

Cadillac, of course, would be Larry Canada's car of choice. This was Canada's turf, the one place in the vicinity of Miami where he could hold a meeting and be reasonably sure of not being monitored or interrupted. It was a little melodramatic, but Canada had always had an excessive streak; a big man, he liked to do things in a big way.

Shayne smiled slightly. Tim Rourke's employers were going to love this.

He moved back to the high step and used the glasses again, looking for Gold's Chrysler or other cars. The magnification picked up a glimmer of light from a window of the control trailer.

He climbed down. Surprising Canada and Gold in a secret conference two days before the opening of bids for a new stretch of highway would be almost enough. It would prove nothing, but the lawyers would then let Rourke print his accumulation of rumors and leaks, and Gold would be laughed at if he attempted to sue.

But it would be better to make this a public event, with other witnesses in addition to a pair of private detectives working for Rourke's paper.

"Fireworks time," he told Frieda softly. "Bicycle back and call the Homestead barracks. Tell them to get some cars out here fast. Somebody's looting the site. Do you have a gun in the van?"

He felt her shake her head no.

"Here, take mine." He put it in her hand. "I'm going to try for a picture. Swing around and come back from the north. Put up a roadblock, barrels, rocks, whatever there is. If one of them wants to leave before the cops get here, he'll have to stop to clear the road. If you have to, shoot out a tire. We want to catch them together."

He touched her shoulder and let her go. That should do it. He could roll one of the trucks out and block the down exit. Neither Cadillacs or Chryslers are rough-country cars.

Moving cautiously, he checked the next piece of equipment, a scraper. It was parked on a slight rise. If he took off the brake and turned hard, it would roll into position to block both lanes with its long, angled blade.

He continued to be extremely careful. Everything about this told him that Canada had come alone. Canada had a reputation for trusting nobody. Probably that was why he had lasted so many years. But Shayne, too, had lasted, and one of the reasons for that was that he took as few chances as possible.

He tried to keep the glimmer of light from the control trailer in sight as he circled, coming down and in. He lost it for a moment, blocked by a long storage trailer. As he came around, he had a sense that the scene had changed, and felt for his glasses.

Now one of the big Euclid payloaders was in his way. He stepped on the bucket yoke and then found an even higher perch against the front of the cab. He was seeing a different trailer window now, and this one had a chink of light along the bottom edge. Something moved. He saw the corner of a desk, part of a control console. A hand appeared, holding a paper. Another hand came into the field. The single papery object turned into several. Envelopes.

Another fragmented headlight beam swept across the tops of the taller machines. Concentrating hard, Shayne almost missed a flicker of movement to the right of the trailer. Swinging, he searched the area.

A figure moved out from the loading bin and approached the parked Cadillac. One hand was extended, groping through what to him was nearly complete darkness. Isolated in Shayne's binoculars, he seemed tall and somewhat misshapen. He was wearing a warm-up suit and a tight-fitting cap. He turned his head. Shayne's hand jerked slightly as a face out of a nightmare jumped at him. It was a mask, the kind of protective mask worn by hockey goalies to keep from being stunned or killed by flying pucks.

Hunched and furtive, the masked figure continued along the Cadillac's long flank. The door opened. He slipped inside.

Shayne's mind was racing. A killing? No, a killer wouldn't hide in the car. Then a kidnapping. Big Larry Canada would bring a far higher price than poor Eddie Maye. That meant there were others hidden in the darkness, waiting for the meeting to end. Other cars. Other guns.

Chapter 8

Downey had found a wrecker equipped with a siren. To make sure it was working, he flicked the switch on and off quickly, producing a spurt of noise. He had also carried in a regulation riot-control bullhorn. Together, these two noisemakers should put both Canada and the Tallahassee bureaucrat into a nice state of panic.

The trio had two hours to prepare. The mercury lights were burning, but a sweep through the site showed them that Downey had been right: the watchman had been told to get lost so Canada could have the place to himself.

Downey assigned roles, and they went through the whole thing twice. So what if Canada and Gold didn't use a trailer, but talked in the car. It would be Canada's car. One scream from that siren, and the Highway Commissioner would leap out and burn rubber getting away. If Canada had a gun, Downey would use the bullhorn and talk him into throwing it out.

"Good God, man," he said when Werner continued to nip at his heels. "You'd think I never made an arrest. These people are realists. When they see they're outnumbered, they come in quietly and call the lawyer."

"But if he brings anybody with him—"

"Wernie, look," Downey said, clearly suffering. "We control. If they come in three cars, we sit here and jack off and wait for some better time. Who's in a hurry? For that much dough, I'm willing to make it a six-month project."

And that was easy for Downey, Pam thought, because he was drawing a city salary. She and Werner had both left their jobs. They had decided not to ask Downey for an advance because that would really put him in charge. Her airplane ticket to New York was her ace in the hole. If she was really turned off by the way things were going, she could always pull out, and it gave her a dreamlike feeling. In dreams, she always escaped by sprouting wings and going straight up.

The hot plant, according to Downey, had been fixed as the meeting place. Downey was guessing that they would go into the superintendent's trailer, a radio-equipped command post for the whole operation. Werner was posted near this trailer, leaning against the fender of a big oil truck. At the first sign of a car, he would drop to the ground and slide between the front wheels. If they were lucky, Canada would park directly across from him.

Downey and Pam were in the wrecker.

"That kid is beginning to get to me," Downey said

in a low voice. "You'd think he was doing us a Goddamn favor. I don't like that la-di-da attitude."

He fingered the siren switch. Pam was glad to see
that even this hardened professional seemed nervous.

"Like to sound you out on something," he said.
"This Werner's our weak link, I mean afterward. Put
him in a room with a light in his eyes, and he's going to
holler for Mommy. I know the type."

"I think he may be tougher than you think."

"Yeah? You, I'm not worried about. You'd spit in
their eye, which is the only thing to do in those cases,
and now I'm talking as a man who's spent twenty-five
years on the far side of the desk. Right now, I admit,
we need him."

He put his hand on the inside of her thigh, well up.
"That movie tonight. Christ Jesus. I've heard they were
raw, but wasn't that something? *There they are,*" he
said suddenly, leaning forward.

A car was coming through the forest of pillars. It
jounced off the pavement onto rougher ground and
headed straight at them, its headlights on fire.

Downey's fingers tightened. "Down."

They went down so fast that their heads bumped.
The headlights swept past the windshield. After a moment, Downey lifted his head. A car door opened, the
headlights went off. Pam didn't like to be the female,
crouching in terror and leaving the decisions to the
man, and she forced herself to look out. She saw an
immense bearded man in a wrinkled white suit, a shirt
with a necktie. He walked to a switch box on one of
the light poles. An instant later, the mercury-vapor
lamps flickered and died.

"There now," Downey breathed. "Didn't I tell you
he'd turn off the lights?"

A light came on in one of the trailers. Pam turned

Downey's wrist so she could see the watch face. It was three minutes to eleven. The Highway Commissioner had driven all the way from Tallahassee, but he arrived exactly on the tick of eleven. He came in another Detroit gas-eating monster. He wheeled it alongside the Cadillac and cut his lights before getting out. They saw him briefly as the trailer door opened. When he was inside, a Venetian blind slammed down, obliterating most of the light.

"Now, Werner, old buddy," Downey said quietly, "don't freeze up on me."

Werner had been told to wait long enough to be sure neither man came back to get something he had forgotten. Minutes passed. In the blackness, it was impossible to tell if he had started or was still lying on his belly under the oil truck, fingernails digging into the dirt. Pam knew that feeling. She had experienced the same thing in Eddie Maye's garage, had stayed in a frozen crouch, unable to move. Now, for some reason, she was anxious for things to happen.

Downey checked the time again and nudged her with an elbow. "Get out and give him a goose." His hand came up hard between her legs. "Do this right and we'll get plastered and have a high old time."

He may have been trying to ease the tension, but it was extremely unsettling and annoying. She trailed her fingertips along the wrecker's side and reached out, waving, until she touched the next truck. Almost at once, she whirled and felt her way back. Downey jumped as the door opened.

"Forgot my damn mask."

She realized that Downey had yanked out his gun. He hadn't fired, at least. She picked the mask off the seat and had her usual difficulty lining up the eye holes. She started off again, furious, sure that other things would be forgotten. Werner was right. There was no point putting themselves through this for a one-third share. One-third was too low.

Her way was strewn with huge obstacles which she had to find her way around. There was a blink of light as the Cadillac's door opened. It blinked off at once. Pam stopped, touching some kind of machine with an enormous, smooth-sided bucket which was partly raised. Briefly there was a faint glow from the Cadillac. Werner was using a tiny flash to find the ignition wire. Then it went dark.

His next move now would be to set the dome-light switch so it wouldn't flash on when the door opened, then soak the cloth pad with chloroform and get down. After that, the plan called for a four-minute wait. In the rehearsals, Downey had made them sit still in a darkened room to get an idea of how fantastically long four minutes can be when nothing is happening.

Now the seconds ticked by. This was ridiculous, Pam thought. Surely Downey had lost track and gone back to zero. Do it, she whispered fiercely. Now!

The siren's scream, when it came, was so sudden and frightening that she had the sensation of being lifted clear of the ground. Her hands flew up, and her knuckles rang against the bucket.

Downey's voice thundered from the bullhorn. "Robinson, you men block that exit right we've got them bottled up here be careful they may be armed they may be armed—"

There were two quick shots.

Holding the night glasses on the Cadillac, Shayne saw the masked figure slip into the back seat and crouch out of sight. Shayne was in a minority here. He had given Frieda his gun. All he could hope to do was keep them occupied until the cops showed up.

At first, when the siren blew, he thought he had misjudged distances and the cops had come by some shorter secondary road. He aimed the camera at the door of the trailer. It was loaded with sensitive film, and when he snapped the shutter, its eye would be all the way open.

The siren had been engineered to penetrate traffic noises and scare slower cars to the side of the road. It was heart-attack music. It didn't quite get to Shayne, who had been expecting something like it, but it worked well on the two men in the trailer, who must have been already considerably on edge. The door flew open, spilling light. One of the men jumped out. It was Gold, the Commissioner. He had a dispatch case swinging in one hand. Shayne snapped a picture, advanced the film, and snapped another as Gold stumbled and went sprawling.

Canada, inside, was standing at the control console, his head cocked. He felt in one drawer, then another, and brought out a gun.

Shayne tried for another picture with both men in it, but he wasn't in time. The light went off.

The man on the ground retrieved his dispatch case and ran to the parked Chrysler. The engine sprang to life. As the car came around, the headlights swept across the trailer and showed Canada in the doorway. Shayne got a shot of that, for what it was worth.

Gold's driving reflexes were ahead of the automatic shift. As the car rocketed away, its rear wheels kicked out a cascade of dirt and gravel. Shayne brought the glasses to bear on the area in front of the trailer. The big man was running, seeming to flutter all over inside his loose clothes. The bullhorn continued to clamor. Canada wrenched open the car door. Something stopped him. Sensing someone's presence in the car or warned by the fact that the overhead light didn't blink on, he stepped quickly to one side.

Hearing the Cadillac door open, Pam thought for an instant that their plan was working. One shift of weight, and the trap would close.

But Canada was wary. Gold's headlights were sliding rapidly north. In another moment, the Chrysler would rejoin the anonymous stream of traffic on the Interstate. So that danger, the danger of being caught here together, was nearly over.

Now it was up to Downey, who claimed to be an expert on persuading criminals to surrender. This they hadn't rehearsed. The siren closed off abruptly. Pam stood absolutely still, listening for movement. She had the impression, without hearing it happen, that Werner had slipped out of the Cadillac.

"Mr. Canada," Downey called on the bullhorn, his tone slightly mocking. "Larry Canada. We saw your Cadillac drive in. If you're here, say something."

There was no answering sound.

"We could shoot you, Mr. Canada. We don't want to do that. We've got a group of professionals here, and just so you'll know I'm not shitting you, I want my people to make some noise."

Pam struck her gun against the bucket. Werner, some distance away, mooed like a cow.

Downey had moved. "You remember Eddie Maye. We did that, Mr. Canada, so you'd know we're serious people. You're the man with the real dough. We wouldn't hurt you for the world."

In the silence that followed, Werner remarked in an

almost conversational tone, "Watch out, he's got a gun."

"But so have we, don't we? If we have to shoot him, make it a flesh wound. Plenty of flesh there to choose from."

Suddenly the mercury lights flashed on. Downey's masked figure stood at the foot of one of the light poles, his hand on the master switch. Werner was out in the open, in front of the Cadillac. He jumped for cover as the fat man, backed up against one of the conveyor belts, fired at him. The lights went off.

"No," Downey called from a new place. "No, no, Mr. Canada. That was foolish, because we're jumpy, you know? We could make a mistake. Think about it a minute. How did we know you'd be out here? We've been getting this ready a long time. We've got a good place to take you. We laid in a lot of steak and bourbon. We know you like lime pies. We got three in the freezer. What the hell, all we want is money. We're going to weigh you, and go for about three thousand bucks a pound. Tell you what I want you to do. I'm going to roll my flashlight out in the open. Toss the gun out where we can see it. You know that's the smart thing to do, the only thing."

A lighted flashlight rolled across the dirt. The spill from its beam showed Werner, to Pam's surprise, on the conveyor belt above Canada, the chloroformed cloth in one hand. Canada whirled and fired, and in two jumps was at the door of the trailer and inside.

"Use your head," the bullhorn shouted. "There's a phone in there, but what good's it going to do you?"

Suddenly there was a thunderclap, a whistle, an immense sigh, and with a tremendous groaning and clanking the big mixer came alive and began to revolve. The belts ran up to the loading hatches empty, and came back empty. It didn't change Canada's situation inside the trailer, but it was a loud announcement that he didn't intend to surrender.

Pam didn't hear Downey approach. He touched her, and a spark jumped between them.

"Cover the door. Shoot him in the leg if he comes out. Keep it low—take your time."

He ripped off his sweat shirt and wadded it into a ball. There was a gas pump several vehicles away. He felt his way to it, gave the sweat shirt a good soaking, then circled to the trailer, keeping low. He smashed a window. A match flared. When the sweat shirt caught, he scooped it up on his gun barrel and threw it in.

Inside, Canada could be seen, his back to the console. Downey yelled, "Go on being stupid. We'll set the trailer on fire, you'll really be cooked. We want to be nice to you. Girls, anything you want, name it."

Nothing else in the trailer had caught, and the blaze was already beginning to die.

"We'll give you a short count," Downey called. "Throw your gun out first. At the count of three, I'm going to strike the Goddamn match."

Canada shook himself and made a placating palms-out gesture. The pistol came spinning into the light. Then the huge figure loomed in the doorway, turned sideward to get down the steps. As he reached the ground, Werner moved in with the chloroform.

Chapter 9

Shayne was watching the action from the high cab of a Euclid payloader. He stepped across to the next vehicle, a bulldozer-backhoe, and turned on its radio. Moving only when the bullhorn was roaring, he went deeper into the park, turning on radios at random. On the return, he stopped to take off the brake of the scraper he had picked out earlier, and let it roll out to block the road. The hot plant began banging and clattering, and he was able to move more freely. He found the ignition key under the floor mat and checked the controls. The bullhorn was calling on Canada to surrender. Canada came out. A masked figure pounced on him from behind, and a second masked man ran up and helped hold him until he slumped to the ground.

The Cadillac's headlights came up. A third figure

appeared. Together they struggled to get their heavy captive into the back seat of the car. Shayne waited. When the job was nearly complete, he picked the transmitter off the dashboard. He looked at the highway for an instant before committing himself, but there was still no sign of reinforcements.

"Hold it," he called harshly. "Right there."

The sudden command traveled from the payloader to all the live radios in a great circle around the Cadillac and came back, echoing from one metallic surface to the next. He had the volume all the way up everywhere, and it produced a pretty effect. One of the figures wheeled back, his gun raised. The words had come from everywhere at once, and there was nobody to shoot.

"Drop your guns," Shayne commanded. "Hands on the hood of the car. All of you."

The man with the gun continued to wheel.

"You told Canada not to be stupid," Shayne said. "Don't be stupid yourself. One wrong move, and you're dead. *Drop the guns. Now.*"

One warning shot might have tipped the balance. The figure in the open lowered his gun without dropping it and dived for the car. The headlights winked off.

All the radios clamored: "Open up when the car moves."

Shayne pressed the starter switch, and the powerful engine came to life as the Cadillac jerked forward. He turned on his headlights. They were oversize, like everything else about the enormous machine. Caught in a blaze of light, the Cadillac came back. It went forward again, heading not for the road Shayne had blocked, but deeper into the site. Shayne had once spent a day in a payloader, checking on a time-sheet swindle, with a driver who could pick up a cigarette butt with a flick of his huge bucket. He had learned the principal moves, but he had to fumble. The bucket lifted and dropped as he got the wrong lever. The machine, he knew, had a top speed of forty miles an hour, but it was slow building up. He couldn't hope to overtake a Detroit car on a straight, smooth road. This track, however, was anything but that. He was in third with two more to go, coming up fast. The Cadillac went slithering far out on a turn. Shayne, with his tight turning radius, came up behind it before it could recover.

He lifted the bucket and threw the wheel over sharply.

The big bucket slammed into the Cadillac's fender, spun the car around, and banged it hard into a parked truck. Shayne was braking and sliding. The bucket's momentum whipped him around. He reversed and came back, bucket down. He turned and set. He lifted the bucket and brought it down with crushing force on the car's front end, sending the rear wheels high in the air. One tire blew.

The nearby radios all shouted at once, "Stay in the car. I want to see three guns."

He saw one at once, thrust out the nearest window. The bullet went through his windshield. He cut the lights and dropped to the ground. He didn't need to capture all three. One would be enough.

He faded back through the parked equipment and began to work toward the Cadillac's taillights, which continued to burn in spite of what had happened to the rest of the car. Almost there, he reached into a truck cab, snapped the headlight knob, and pushed it back in at once, having seen one of the masked figures on top of a bulldozer blade. Shayne ran straight at him in the darkness, colliding with him as he came down. Shayne had the advantage. He knew it was an enemy, but before the other could shoot, he had to be sure that Shayne wasn't one of his colleagues.

Shayne chopped hard at a forearm and heard the gun land some distance away. Getting the man around the chest, Shayne ran him backward. They had to collide with something soon, and they did—the side of a truck. The curve of the fender caught his opponent at the base of his spine. He gave a high squeal of pain or dismay. As his head came forward, Shayne clubbed him with a hard rising left. The heavy mask took the force out of the blow. The tight cap came off in Shayne's hand, and he had an impression of an abundance of hair. He went to the body, getting in two punishing punches before he was caught on the back of the head with something hard swung with considerable force.

He went down, already starting his roll. He pivoted and went under the truck.

"Here!" somebody shouted.

As he came back out, Shayne banged against a moving body. They grappled for an instant. Something touched him on the side of the face, unmistakably the muzzle of a gun.

All the lights flashed on at once. There were too many guns in this fight, all on the wrong side, and Shayne went back under the truck. He saw running feet, a masked face, a gun.

He struck his shoulder painfully against the hump of the axle as he rolled. Another gun went off somewhere else, and the figure looking in at Shayne pitched sideward, making a hurt sound. A hand came down and pulled him to his feet. Shayne counted legs. He got to five. There must have been one more he missed.

He pulled around, seeing movement in another direction, and saw a bicycle wheel. Frieda was back. He waited for her to find him.

The others were moving away. After a time, she called his name softly. Crawling out, he went toward the sound. They met at the wrecked car.

"Three of them. You hit one. Where the hell are the cops?"

"Coming."

Taking her hand, he pulled her to the payloader. In the high cab, he started the engine but left the headlights off, and picked up the transmitter.

His own words came rushing back at them from all sides. "Give up. There's no way you'll get out of this. Give up."

"I'm impressed," Frieda said when silence returned. "Why aren't they?"

"I heard them say they killed somebody. So they're going to try to get by us. What happened with Gold?"

"I couldn't stop him, Mike. He went straight through the barrier. Caved in the whole front end, but he kept going."

"Here they come," Shayne said, bringing up the lights. "Give them a couple of shots to keep their heads in."

Shayne had guessed the direction wrong. The payloader had four gears in reverse. He started at the top of the range instead of the bottom and stalled. The other vehicle, a light-duty tow truck, was headed away from the highway. Shayne came about and ran up quickly through the forward gears. The tow truck hit a swinging gate and went through without slowing.

"We won't catch them in this," Frieda said.

"I don't see anything faster."

He reversed and backed up to the control trailer. Inside, he turned on the lights and found the phone.

He had to look up the number. After that, he listened to the phone ring for some time before a voice said, "Highway Patrol."

"You got a call about a break-in at the Homestead construction site. They're in a tow truck traveling east on a dirt road out of the interchange. The road's not on the map. It must come out by the air base. Three people, and they're armed."

"The trouble is," the voice said, "I already dispatched all the cars. They're coming in from two sides. I know that road, but I couldn't get anybody in there in time to cut them off. Who is this calling?"

Shayne replaced the phone slowly.

"No?" Frieda said from the doorway.

"Too late. But that's all right. We know a couple of new things, and we have Canada."

"We have Canada," Frieda repeated. "What good does that do?"

"When he wakes up, he'll think we're the ones who kidnapped him. That opens up all kinds of interesting possibilities. Let's get him out of here."

Frieda went for the van while Shayne examined the Cadillac. The blows from the bucket had knocked the body out of square, and neither of the rear doors would open. Canada was firmly wedged between the two seats. He was giving off a strong smell of chloroform. Shayne was about to back out. Then he leaned all the way in and picked an empty syringe off the floor. He sniffed it. If Canada had been given a full load of this, he would be out for the rest of the night.

At first, Shayne considered getting a wrecker and taking the whole car. That would still leave the problem of getting the big man out somewhere else, so he swung the payloader into position, coming in at an angle with the bucket all the way down. The sharp front lip dug deep beneath one of the Cadillac's rear tires. Shayne lifted straight up, flipping the big car over on its side. Then he raised the bucket, lowered it onto the car, and stepped up the downward pressure slowly, checking at intervals until the body was back in square. He unslung a long double chain and hooked it to the frame between front and rear doors. He lifted; the Cadillac came up easily, not exactly in balance. The door could be opened now, but Canada was still jammed. Shayne remembered a jerking technique which the operator had used to shake sticky materials out of the bucket. He swung the big car over a sand pile and jerked the lifting lever forward and back quickly, producing a powerful grating shake. The Cadillac danced and jangled at the end of the chain. After the second shake, Canada came tumbling out to a soft landing in the sand.

Shayne was getting the hang of it now. He worked the lever again, dropping the bucket sharply, which dislodged the hook. The Cadillac, like a mouse tossed by a cat, flew through the air and ended up on the gravel bank. At that point, it had probably lost most of its resale value.

"A marvelous toy," Frieda called up. "And we ought to be going, Mike."

Shayne meanwhile had continued to improve on his original idea. He turned the bucket completely upside down, swung hard, and caved in one corner of the big equipment trailer, partially jarring it off its blocks. He worked the bucket edge into the opening and came back, peeling off one of the side panels. He tilted the bucket forward. Jumping down, he climbed into the trailer, which was brightly illuminated by the payloader's headlights. He gutted it completely, throwing everything into the bucket—torches, jackhammers, welding machines, drills, hand tools, one huge payloader wheel and tire. Frieda had the van in position with the rear doors open. Shayne swung the bucket and tipped it all in.

Then he picked up Canada, getting a good deal of sand in the same bite. He tilted the bucket slowly. When Canada started to slide, Frieda guided him into the van.

The back of the van had two fitted bunks, a small stove, and a smaller ice chest. Shayne raised one of the bunks, moved the fat man underneath, and lowered the bunk again. The clutter of stolen equipment around him would keep him from rolling.

"Well, I don't get it," Frieda said, "but unless we want to meet those police cars on the highway—"

"We're going out the back door."

He pointed at the dirt road the others had used. At the gate, she paused briefly while Shayne looked at the lock. It had been clipped off with bolt cutters. They drove on. Seeing the first revolving light behind her, she braked sharply and cut her own headlights.

"You better drive, Mike," she said after a moment. "I can't see a thing."

"I'll lead you."

He found a small pencil flash in the glove box. Jumping down, he set off at a fast walk. When they reached a line of trees, he came back in the van and she turned on the lights.

Almost at once, they came to the empty tow truck, abandoned at the side of the road.

"Here's where they changed cars," Shayne said. "Don't stop. I want to be back on a paved road before they start talking about us on the shortwave."

"Next time we rob a construction site," Frieda said, "let's take a payloader. They'd make lovely pets."

With its heavy load, the van was giving them a surprisingly stable ride. Sometimes, even on pavement, it had a slight tendency to wander. The road gradually improved, skirting the Homestead Air Base, and came out on Route 1.

"Now can we talk?" Frieda said, relaxing. "I think I'm beginning to see the idea. Canada's gone. So is a lot of their portable equipment. What the real kidnappers are going to think—"

"Right. That wasn't a rescue, but a hijacking. According to Tim, there's been some pretty heavy pilfering going on. They'll think the regular thieves were working tonight, saw what was happening to Canada, and decided on the spur of the moment to move in. But this was a well-planned operation. When Canada didn't cooperate, they reacted nicely. They've probably got the ransom note written, all their arrangements made. They've been thinking about how they're going to invest all that money. I don't think they'll give up as long as they think there's a chance to recover. If they can find out who's been doing the stealing—"

"They'll try a hijack in reverse, and we'll be there waiting for them. Clever. But how will they know anything's missing? They were already gone when you did all that."

"A couple of angles I haven't told you about yet. They already kidnapped one guy and killed him—a loan shark named Eddie Maye. Eddie's wife told us he was being followed by a cop. How big a cop we don't know, but he must have been fairly big because Eddie was lying awake worrying about him. That voice on the bullhorn sounded pretty professional, a cop's voice. He'll be talking to the sheriff. And then he'll ask around—who's been doing the stealing out here?"

Chapter 10

Werner peeled off his goalie's mask and slapped it against the dashboard.

"Strictly according to plan. Everything taken care of. What could possibly go wrong?"

"Now don't bug me, boy," Downey warned. "I've taken all the shit from you I'm going to take. I've had the full quota."

"Stop it," Pam said, but her tone showed that she didn't expect anybody to pay attention to *her*.

Werner had torn the sweat shirt back from his shoulder wound. One look had told Downey that the bullet had nipped in and out without catching anything but flesh and muscle. But naturally the boy thought he was on the point of dying.

Downey brought the tow truck to a sliding stop

where they had left the cars. "Go straight to the Heights house," he said curtly. "I'll be with you in an hour, probably."

"We won't wait up," Werner said.

"I'm going back in as a police officer and find out what's going on. Something funny, I can guarantee you that."

"No more!" Werner shouted, suddenly furious. "We've had enough, do you understand?"

"Come on, we have to talk about it."

"No more!" Werner shouted again. "You shit head, you know what you did? You nearly got us all killed!"

Downey slapped his hand away and started the motor. Didn't they understand they were like olives in a bottle here? First they had to scatter. Then they had to meet for the post-mortem. They couldn't leave these loose ends flying around.

He got off fast. They would realize soon enough that they could air their grievances inside four walls, not out here where they might be seen and remembered by a couple of teen-agers who had been to an X-rated movie and were looking for seclusion to do their own screwing.

He heard a police siren. He didn't believe it at first. How could they know? He listened more intently. That was what it definitely was, a siren, but it came from the Interstate.

Werner, driving like a madman in his Ford, came up behind him, honking, headlights up full. He rode up to Downey's car and clashed bumpers. On top of everything else, with that shoulder he had to be driving one-handed. A wipe-out here would be good news, wouldn't it? Downey speeded up to establish an interval, got on a better road, and lost them. They had paid a month's rent on a house in Miami Heights, back from the bay with trees around it and no close neighbors. They'd be sensible and go there and wait, wouldn't they? Sure they would.

As a matter of fact, for kids, they had done pretty well. Downey remembered the first time someone had shot at him. He hadn't liked it much, either. He had hit the pavement so fast he skinned his whole face, the first blood he had lost as a cop. And that reminded him that he was a cop still, with a cop's privileges. He turned on the police band. A couple of highway cruisers were talking to each other. A *robbery?* Robbery, hell. That was a snatch, man, interrupted by persons unknown, one armed with a gun, one with a payloader.

He slowed down until he was barely crawling. The dispatcher had pulled off one of the cars to look for a tow truck. That worried Downey. How would they know about a tow truck unless somebody saw it, and in that case what else had they seen? Of course, the masks had still been on then. Coming to a full stop on the shoulder, he felt for the pint bottle in his glove compartment. As a matter of fact, he was damn tired. For the last couple of weeks, he had been working full-time at a regular job and full-time on this. He had had to do all the planning, all the psychology. The size of the stake had added to the strain. His two colleagues, he was discovering, were far from being the most transparent people in the world. With Pam especially, he could never be sure what she was thinking. He impressed her, he knew. At the same time, he had a strong suspicion that she thought he was a bit of a phony.

He couldn't understand Canada's behavior. The part called for him to put down his gun and come out laughing. Why all the shooting? True, they had shot Eddie Maye, but they wouldn't shoot Canada because he had to be delivered alive. And all those voices suddenly. Downey had been in some hairy situations in his time, especially during those years in the black precinct, but being attacked by a payloader was one of the worst. Usually a Cadillac gives you a feeling of security and power. Not this time. He could still see that big bucket lift, lift, lift fifteen feet in the air and come smashing down.

The whiskey burned some of the fuzziness away, and he took another bite. If Werner hadn't run off the minute he was nicked, Downey could have turned on the lights and found out what they were up against. It couldn't have been cops. They hadn't behaved like cops, and from what he was hearing on the police band, the cops were just beginning to get there now. Canada's people? No, there would have been more gunfire, Downey would now be lying there dead probably, and the cops would never have been notified at all.

So by God, maybe two things had been running concurrently there, their own thing and the robbery the cops were talking about. It would have to be somebody who knew the site and knew how to run a payloader. Two people at the most, amateurs, doing a little harmless picking on their own time. All that radio commotion might have come from a single source. Could it be? It could be, Downey decided. A couple of guys sitting there in the darkness, getting more and more itchy, and when they saw that what was happening was a snatch of Big Larry Canada, easily a million-dollar parcel, they decided to make a little racket with the radios and see what happened.

He drove to the site, identified himself to the patrolmen, said he had picked up their conversation, and could he do anything to help? They couldn't think of anything. He wandered away and looked for the Cadillac. That long, arrogant car, perched halfway up a little volcano of gravel, was surely a mess. Canada, as he had supposed, was no longer inside.

"Now how the hell did *that* happen?" he asked.

The highway patrolmen, who saw plenty of wrecked cars in the course of their working day, hadn't been able to explain this one. Somebody happened to know that the job super lived in a trailer in the big encampment outside of Leisure City. They did some phoning. When the super arrived, the first thing he was able to do was identify the smashed car as belonging to the top boss. Everybody suddenly became much more careful. One of the sheriff's deputies, who had found a bottle of whiskey in the trailer and was about to see how it tasted, replaced the cap and put it back in the drawer.

The super exclaimed when he saw the looted trailer. Downey went inside with him. The super couldn't believe the extent of the loss. Usually it was one or two small pieces, more on the order of petty pilfering. This had been done by professionals. On the other hand, the insurance company had been getting fed up with the incessant nibbling losses, so maybe the pricks had decided to go for a big score before more stringent security measures made it harder or impossible. A payloader tire had been taken. Mounted, one of those babies would set you back something like a thousand and a half. You couldn't walk out with one in your back pocket.

When Downey attempted to get a little more—had they ever caught anyone taking, for example?—the man closed up. That would have to come from the office.

Never mind. Downey had already thought of somebody who was sure to know.

Soupy Simpson, a well-known street figure in North-west Miami, was built like an ex-jockey who has stopped starving himself to make weight. His bones were as light as a chicken's. In periods when the money was good and he didn't have to choose between food and heroin (heroin won), he put on weight around the middle. He usually seemed cool and easy, even cheerful, as though nothing bad could possibly happen to him. Much already had. He led a hazardous life. He was a fence, a gifted middleman who was will-ing to peddle any kind of stolen property if the margin was right. Because of his high expenses, he also had to moonlight by selling news and gossip. For this mer-chandise, his customers were the police, an occasional newspaperman like Tim Rourke of the *News*. This didn't pay much, but it often made the difference be-tween a bad night and going to bed happy.

He slept in a bowling-alley shoe room. Turkey, who ran the place, was still at the front desk. Suddenly Tur-key began coughing hard. He had a cigarette smoker's cough anyway, but this was more and it meant they had visitors. Simpson swept his materials into a cha-mois bag. The top sash of his single window was down a few inches. Standing on the cot, he dislodged a taut elastic, hooked it into the bag, and let go. The bag left the room fast, coming to rest outside, high up under the eaves.

He was back on the cot taking off his socks when a city detective named Jack Downey walked in. At this time of night, Downey was bad news. Nevertheless Simpson's face split open in a wide, friendly grin, and he put out his hand.

"Hey, Jack, I'm honored."

Downey was one of those cops it is impossible to like.

He was a Godfather expert, with charts all over the walls of his office. Simpson and the others in his stable of snitches kept him contented by screening him from anything that would contradict his ideas. When a loan shark named Eddie Maye turned up dead, for example, Simpson told Downey it was an episode in a power struggle between organized crime families, although everybody knew it was actually a kidnapping attempt that had gone bad.

Downey was in a rotten mood. Instead of taking Simpson's hand, he put three glassine envelopes in it. Simpson looked down in surprise.

"I do hope this isn't a bust," he said gently.

"That remains to be seen." His tone and manner were equally grating. Whatever his standing elsewhere, in this room he unquestionably had the power. "I want a few answers, and I don't have time for the usual bullshit."

He swung over a straight chair, the only one in the room, and sat down. Simpson managed to stay relaxed, but he didn't like the visit. The time of night by itself made it important.

"Homestead," Downey said. "Pilfering. The construction site on the Interstate. What do you know about that?"

Simpson was liking this less and less. Homestead was sheriff's country, and the sheriff was touchy about Miami cops who didn't stay in their own jurisdiction.

"Why are you interested, Jack? Homestead is out of your territory."

"Larry Canada is my territory, I go where he takes me. Let's hear a yes or a no. Can you help me?"

"Jack—maybe," Simpson said, twisting. "I know it goes on."

Downey lit a cigarette, forgetting to offer one to the man on the cot. "Who are they? How do they fence it?"

"I don't know names and addresses, Jack. These are small guys by definition. They work for a living. It's something they scoop on the side."

"I told you I don't have time for the bullshit. Don't try to Jew me up."

Simpson stopped smiling. He had had some unhappy experiences with Irishmen whose eyebrows came close to meeting over their nose. This could be a very mean man. He exaggerated his agitation slightly to give Downey a sense that the menace had been understood.

"You say Canada. He has a piece of everything out there, never mind that it's small, because of the principle of the thing. And if it gets back to Larry that we were talking about him, I could be in serious trouble. You know I live from day to day."

"I'm not asking about selling the stuff back later. That's between Canada and his insurance. All I want to know is stage one and stage two. Small guys, I agree. Those kind of names are in the public domain."

Simpson continued to twist, fingers laced in his lap, and Downey's eyebrows approached each other and touched. "What are you trying to tell me? That I can't bust you right now for possession?"

"No, no. If I knew off the top of my head, would be one thing. I'll have to make a phone call, and they'll remember it was Simpson was asking."

Downey took out three more little envelopes and added them to the pile on Simpson's knee. He really must want this information. Usually he paid cash out of the informers' budget. So it couldn't be regular police business. The police–informer tie is like a marriage. To work, it must go both ways. The cop needs to know what his snitch is up to, to keep him in line. And the reverse is true. For a really solid relationship, the snitch, too, needs a handle.

"Give me a couple of minutes, if I can locate the bastard. He sleeps different places."

Downey's expression continued to threaten, telling Soupy that if he tried to evaporate or come back without the information, he was not only going to get arrested, he was going to have the shit kicked out of him for resisting arrest. Part of the cop mystique is getting a chance to bloody your knuckles now and then.

Simpson went out to the office, where his friend was worrying about him.

"Give me a shot of booze," he said urgently. Turkey got out the bottle and poured. "Heavy stuff in there. I'd like to know what he's into."

"I don't like him coming around."

"I love it myself."

He folded himself in the phone booth and took the phone off the hook in case Downey looked out. After a certain amount of time, he went back and told Downey what he wanted to know. There were two regular thieves, Rusty Benjamin and a truck driver named Vaughan. His informant didn't know if Vaughan was a first name or a last name. They lived in a big trailer park seven or eight miles south of the new interchange, near Leisure City. Apparently the set-up was this. They had their own camper there, and they rented a trailer from the park under a fake name. Whatever they brought back from work, they stuck in this second trailer. The whole point was not to take much at one time, so it didn't pay a fence to keep in day-to-day touch. As soon as they accumulated a fair-sized load, they notified the buyer, who came with his own vehicle, hooked onto the trailer, and took it away, bringing it back empty the next morning. They got their money through the mail.

All this was true. The one fact Simpson suppressed was that he himself was the link between the guys and their buyer. Downey didn't need to know that. Downey's eyebrows moved a fraction of an inch further apart, which meant he was satisfied, even though for once Simpson hadn't given him a Mafia connection.

He left. He had been gone only a few minutes when Turkey began coughing again. Simpson swept Downey's envelopes under the mattress, although for all he knew they contained nothing but milk sugar, and was ready for his next guests, who turned out to be Tim Rourke and Mike Shayne, the detective.

Simpson was sort of a friend of these guys, though nobody with his lifestyle could really afford to be friends with anybody. He knew where he was with them. If he didn't want to do business, he said no, and they accepted it.

"Tim, how's the crusade?" he said with his big smile. "Larry Canada's still walking around loose, I'm sorry to see."

"We're working on it," Rourke said.

"You'll never get that guy. Coffee? Turkey just made a fresh pot. A drink maybe?"

"We have some hot construction equipment we want to unload," Shayne said. "It has to be moved fast, and you get the whole take. Do you want it?"

"Sure," Simpson said agreeably, "after you tell me what you're getting me into. Sit down, fellows. You may be in a big rush, but this is the time of night when I begin to go slow."

Shayne took the chair. Rourke, too nervous to sit still, continued to circle. If Simpson had been a fox, his ears would be standing straight up, his mustache would be vibrating. He smelled money, and of course he also smelled trouble. If they said this hot load came from Homestead—

"You're an odds man, Soupy," Shayne said. "What do you think the odds are we can stop that Everglades link-up?"

"The big four-lane? Too much going for it, man. I admit you've surprised me a few times, but even so— well, twenty to one?"

Shayne snorted. "Always nice to talk to you, Soupy. Yeah, I'd say about twenty to one. But we're trying various things, and maybe we'll come up with something. This one's a little far-out. Canada's Homestead job was hit tonight. I happened to walk in on it."

"I don't suppose you want to tell me what you were doing out there?"

"Soupy, some of this it would be healthier not to know. You might be tempted to sell it, and that could get complicated."

"And unhealthy," Simpson agreed. "What kind of values are we talking about?"

"To you, a couple of thousand at the most. We want you to put it in the pipeline so we can see where it goes."

"Like an X-ray," Rourke explained, "where you inject something and take a series of pictures. Soupy, time's going by."

"It can't wait till morning?"

"It was stolen tonight," Shayne said. "We want to peddle it tonight."

"They're going to wonder why I don't get rid of it direct."

"Because you want to keep the connection, keep them satisfied. Cut down the risk. You don't want to be driving the truck and get stopped for a faulty tail-light."

Simpson considered. "They might go for that. How would this be? I've got the key to an empty storefront. You can unload it there. I'll call the guys to come pick it up. That's a round trip of about an hour. Would that fit your schedule?"

"Fine."

And where did Jack Downey fit into this? Simpson had a fleeting impulse to tell Shayne that somebody else was interested in those two guys, Benjamin and Vaughan. He suppressed it. He had to think of himself, and this was turbulent water.

"You were talking about odds," he said. "If I do it, what are the odds I'll get hurt?"

"Four to one."

That jolted a laugh out of Simpson. "Anybody else would say a hundred, and I wouldn't believe it. O.K., I'll do it. Let's see what you have."

Chapter 11

To Lou DeLuca, Canada's ambition to make it big in legitimate business was like a whore's dream of a little house in the suburbs, with a pastel door and a swimming pool. It wasn't a practical thing. To be practical, the only security was to work with the cops, providing the services the public wanted and needed, and to stay the hell out of the headlines. Dope, bets, women—this was nickel-and-dime stuff to Canada. Sure, but how those nickels and dimes added up!

Canada was always in evidence. When he went anywhere, he was noticed. He gave too many big flashy parties. It tickled him when officers of the medical and bar associations and Chamber of Commerce came on his boat. But at the first sign of bad weather, DeLuca had told him again and again, those would be just the people who wouldn't be returning his phone calls. They had their own ass to look after.

So Canada had to go. But it had to be done right. An old-fashioned bang-bang would hurt everybody. What most people wanted was peace and tranquillity, no heat, no hassle, an atmosphere in which they could continue to make a modest living without letting the IRS know the details. There were always a few sore-heads around, and DeLuca had been working on them. But as for people who would go all the way, he had only a handful. Canada, too, had been neglecting this side of it. Times had changed, he kept saying. Horse-shit. Sometimes there was only one thing to do, when you came down to it—stop talking and shoot.

And Eddie Maye had been shot. That had been faked to look like a kidnapping, but Canada must have learned that Eddie was conspiring to get rid of him, and he had moved first. DeLuca had to assume that Eddie had talked freely before taking that shot in the head. So DeLuca was staying close, and he had im-ported two professional shooters from New York.

That committed him to the action. Canada had con-nections in New York, and sooner or later he would hear about it. The trouble was, nothing was ready. Ed-die Maye had promised to set it up, delivering Canada to some certain spot at a certain time. Now that Eddie was no longer around, DeLuca had to think of some other way.

He liked to get off to an early start in the morning, and he liked his eight hours. Nobody called him at night unless it was really important. So when the phone rang after midnight, he came awake in a hurry and grabbed it.

It was Canada's wife, Molly. She wasn't as massive

as her husband, but she ate much of the same cooking, and she showed it, especially between the knees and waist. Now and then, she had given DeLuca a certain look, to the effect that she might be willing to go upstairs with somebody who made regular trips to the gym and kept himself in good shape. He hadn't followed it up, though it remained in the back of his mind.

"Lou, something scary has happened. You've got to help me."

"Sure, Molly." He felt for the .38-caliber bullet he always carried as a good luck piece, a nice reassuring shape. A fatal accident to Canada right now would solve most of his problems, as well as save the hitmen's fees. "Tell me."

"I took a pill, my head's just going around. What was he doing out there, anyway, this late at night?"

"Molly, can you sort of grab hold of yourself? What was this, a phone call?"

"From Homestead. They had a robbery at the site, lots of things taken. And the first thing the police saw when they got there was Larry's car all smashed up."

DeLuca took a half second to drain the eagerness out of his voice. "Was Larry in it?"

"No, that's the thing. It was all bashed in, a total wreck, and no sign of Larry at all! Vanished! Lou, what do you think? Whoever it was talking, some lieutenant, thought maybe Larry got wind of the robbery—but does that sound like him? To go out there all by himself? You know it doesn't."

"When did you see him, for supper?"

"Yes, he ate here, silent as usual, and then he got in the car and went. He's so busy I hardly ever see him at night these days. He's been upset about something. I know, because when he's worried he eats like a real pig. Have you heard anything?" Her voice caught. "Do you think he's been killed?"

"Now what makes you say that? Of course he hasn't been killed, or he'd be there in the car. Hauling Larry around would be no joke, believe me. Put it out of your mind."

"Or kidnapped? That's one of the things I've been terrified of, those stories in the papers. He's so secretive about money. They found a rag soaked in chloroform."

"That's it, then," DeLuca said, already beginning to think what he could do with this. "That isn't too bad. Got him out there on some pretext. Can you stay awake now, do you think?"

"My God, after this do you think I could sleep?"

"Drink lots of coffee. They may want to get in touch right away. Let's definitely figure a kidnapping. It won't be anything long-drawn-out, a matter of days. In and out fast is the idea. I'm going out there now and see what I can pick up. If you get anything more, call my answering service."

He didn't want her to notify anybody else until he found out what was what. "Keep the line open for incoming calls. I'll keep you up to date, trust me. Molly, I'll tell you this. You're one brave woman."

Greco and Nick had never worked together before. Nick was an old face from the neighborhood, and they had no trouble getting along. They enjoyed the same things and kept the same hours. They were being paid for their time, and the client wouldn't like it if he was ready to go and one of them couldn't be reached. So they did everything in pairs, in no hurry for the wait to come to an end. This was the vacation capital of

America, they were staying in the Doral at the client's expense, and Greco had the names of a couple of ho's. Theoretically they were supposed to stay razor-sharp at all times, but tonight when the girls finished work they dropped in with a bit of cocaine.

"No-o," Greco said. "In case we get called out, you know, Nick?"

But they laughed him out of it.

Nick was something of a goof-off, and he kept the girls laughing. He was six-three, with a long skinny neck and an Adam's apple that ran up and down. This was his first time out of New York, except to the Catskills. The Doral wowed him. Greco liked that. He was two years older. He had been to Miami twice, once with an older woman, once with a man.

DeLuca called from the lobby. Nick was nearest the phone, but he was busy just then, and Greco answered. He knew at once, from the abruptness, that they were about to start earning their money.

"Be right there." He hung up. "Nick, this is for us."

Nick claimed he would only take another minute, but Greco made him get up in spite of complaints from the girls. He took one backward step and sat down on the floor.

"Talk about dizzy."

"You've got about one minute to stop being dizzy," Greco told him sternly. "We're going to be driving a car."

"Oh, put me in a car and point me, I'll be O.K."

But before he could get in a car, he had to get off the floor and into the bathroom, where Greco let him stand under a stinging cold shower for a minute or two. Greco himself was weaving ever so slightly. If he relaxed his concentration for an instant, everything ran together like a punctured egg. He wasn't afraid of action. The momentum would keep him going. But if he had to sit waiting for somebody, it would be hell staying awake.

Nick wandered out of the bathroom still wet. The girls thought he was trying to entertain them by the way he kept getting his arms in the wrong sleeves and doing up the buttons in the wrong order. As soon as he was more or less dressed, Greco took the small airlines bag to the bathroom.

"Nick, got something for you."

Nick was trying, Greco would say that for him. He stuck the gun in his waistband under his loose Mexican shirt. As he went back to the bedroom, the gun popped out and dropped to the carpet.

The girls became serious all at once. One of them said, "Uh-oh." The other, named Linda, bounced out of bed and ran to Greco. "I want to come. I never saw one. I won't get in the way. I'll just be, you know, part of the wallpaper."

"Don't be dumb."

"I mean it. I can get dressed in a hurry. Let me! I'll drive."

"We've already got one driver," Nick said, "so shut up before I clout you."

"Nick-y."

She kept begging them as they tried to finish, and Nick had to give her a backhand, which sent her tumbling. The gun popped out again.

"We'll be back," Greco told the girls. "Stay wet."

Nick walked to the elevator with the help of one wall. "I'll tell you this, I've felt better."

"You'll be O.K.," Greco assured him.

In the elevator, Nick straightened to his full height and gave him a good smile. But the elevator went down much too fast and put Nick out on the garage level with everything sagging. He wanted to drive to prove it was possible, but Greco refused to commit suicide. He made the turns carefully. With a gun in his pocket, he was stopping for red lights, although there was little cross traffic. DeLuca was parked on Collins near Fortieth. He got out of his own car and into theirs. He was wearing dark glasses, which Greco considered an affectation at this time of night. He was totally sober. Good God, was he sober! Nick kept staring straight ahead, rocking against the seat belt. He might have been sleeping. A little sleep would do him good, as long as he had the common sense not to snore.

DeLuca's directions took them across a long causeway into Miami proper. A little later, they drew up in front of a bowling alley in a cheap neighborhood.

"The guy's name is Soupy Simpson," DeLuca said. "He's going to give you some information. A couple of names, and where you can find them. Tell him Homestead. Tell him construction shit, tools and like that. Who's been taking? You may have to slap it out of him. That's all right, too. Nick, are you listening?"

"He just dropped off for a minute," Greco said, giving his friend a hard push. "Wake up, stupid."

Downey explained it again on the way to the trailer park.

"I don't know this particular place, but I know the way they're set up. There'll be a transient section for campers and vans. You can come in your own trailer or rent one of theirs. I have a good reason to be out here asking questions. I'm an eager cop, chasing a lead before it cools out. So I'm going in with everything up front and show them the badge."

Werner's shoulder was bandaged. He was babying

that arm, not saying much. Pam had surprised Downey
by instantly agreeing that they had no choice. They
had to check it out. They had committed some crimes
to get this far. They had changed their whole personal-
ities. Then somebody else, who had made no investment at all, had walked off with the prize. Total amateurs, a couple of petty thieves. Without a payloader to
play with, they couldn't be dangerous. She only had
one question. If these thieves really had Canada, would
they take him to a trailer park where vehicles were
parked elbow to elbow and everybody must know each
other?

Downey had made up his mind that that was just
where they'd take him. They had nothing prepared.
And this was a going arrangement, so Canada could be
handled as one more piece of stolen property, more
valuable than most. He would be tied up and gagged,
with his head in a sack. The lack of privacy was all to
the good. It was a huge place. Vehicles came and went.
Rents were paid in advance so transients could leave
before daybreak. Motors would start, lights would
come on. No one would notice or remember.

They passed through Leisure City, following signs.
The park was an eighth of a mile from the highway.
Huge, it certainly was. This was the picking season,
and one section had been reserved for migrants. The
semipermanent trailers were set on blocks, with a parking space between them for a single car. It was impres-
sive, if only as an efficient use of every inch of availa-
ble space.

The office was closed. Downey hammered on the
door. When a cross old man came out to see what he
wanted, Downey showed his Miami badge and was allowed a look at the register.

Then they penetrated the encampment, found the

cross street they wanted, and looked for the number. A trailer was there, but not the pickup that went with it.

"I guess they haven't got back yet," Downey said. "I don't know if that's good or bad. If they didn't bring him, we'll hang them up by their feet and shake it out of them."

A rig turned in from the highway a few minutes later, a pickup pulling a house trailer.

"Let's get parked," Downey said. "A pickup—that could be them."

They were motionless, and consequently, Downey hoped, fairly invisible, when the pickup and trailer combination lumbered on in. There were two men in the cab, one with red hair. They turned into a different street, moving almost to the end of the line before dropping the trailer. Then, instead of parking there, they returned to the berth that had been rented by Benjamin and Vaughan.

"Our guys," Downey said. "If Canada's in that trailer, this is going to be easy."

"If," Werner said from the back seat, his first word in some time.

In Homestead and along the county roads to the south and east, the fiddlers and pickers had put their instruments away for the night. The last drinkers were returning to the park for a few hours sleep before stumbling off to another day in the fields and on the machines. When Shayne saw the pickup and trailer come in from the highway, he shook Rourke awake.

"Mike?" Rourke said, sitting up. "Went to sleep for a minute. Did you say something?"

"They're back with the stuff Soupy sold them. Do you remember what we're doing out here?"

"I think so," Rourke said, scratching. "We're after

the guys who were trying to snatch Canada, only you and Frieda snatched him instead. And they think you're really two other guys—wait, I'll get it in a minute."

"That's close enough. The two other guys who have the rip-off concession at the site, and here they come."

"Except that Canada—"

"Is here with us, sound asleep, instead of in the trailer where the kidnappers think he is. You've got it. Can you stay awake?"

"If that's coffee I smell."

"Just made," Frieda said.

"Mike, tell me again what you want me to do, so I'll be sure I have it straight."

"You're the back-up man. Frieda and I are going to be in the trailer. We'll set it up to fit the story. If I'm wrong about all this, or if I'm right and they don't fall for it, or if something happens to scare them off, we'll waste the night. On the other hand, if it works, it ought to work all the way. They'll come in one at a time, and we can handle up to three. If you see more than three, let's get some cops. Don't go back to sleep."

"Have I ever gone to sleep when I was supposed to stay awake? Well, once or twice maybe, but never in anything this important."

Keeping low, Shayne and Frieda zigzagged cautiously across the chessboard of parked cars. She had pulled on a loose sweater, which hid the shoulder holster. She still wore her perky fisherman's cap. Shayne worked on the door with his picking equipment and small light. When he had it open, she joined him inside.

The huge payloader wheel occupied much of the floor-to-ceiling space in the main room. The rest of the loot from the Homestead robbery had been neatly stowed in closets and under beds. Using only the pencil flash and being careful with that, they set the scene. Frieda had brought a sleeping bag from the van. They stuffed it with pillows to give the illusion of Canada's bulk and roped it to one of the beds. Shayne raised the blind in that bedroom just enough so someone outside could look in and see something on the bed that looked like the prisoner, doped up and helpless.

Then they settled down for the wait.

After the first letdown, which had lasted a couple of hours, Downey was feeling lucky again. He liked it when he followed a hunch and the hunch paid off. He had interpreted that scene at the construction site with a professional eye. He had gone straight to the one man in Miami who could tell him what he wanted to know, the identity of the officially sanctioned thieves. He was now one hundred percent certain that Larry Canada, with a million-dollar price tag tied to his big toe, was parked inside that trailer, a valuable piece of property waiting to be hijacked back. He *had* to be there. No other possibility fitted the facts. But because the two people in his party were still somewhat skeptical, he made one final reconnaissance. The amateurs they were up against had made a typically amateurish mistake, leaving one of the slatted blinds in the trailer only partially drawn. He looked in carefully. It was Canada, all right, zipped up in a mummy bag. Those contours were unmistakable.

Now there were various ways they could do this. Using the outside booth near the office, he called the nearest barracks, who wanted to know who was calling so they could write it down. He told them to forget that, he didn't want to end up in the bay with his feet in concrete. What he had for them was this. Certain people at the Leisure City trailer park had picked up a shipment of high-quality Venezuelan brown in Key West. They had already disposed of much of it, but there was enough left to make a nice seizure for somebody. If they were willing to invest the time, he was willing to give them names and the license plate of their camper because he had been stiffed out of his share of what should have been a lucrative deal.

Earlier, Downey had drawn on his personal cache for the negotiation with Simpson. He had a horror of the stuff personally, but sometimes it was the only way to get information. He had another three ounces in a manila envelope in his car. Benjamin and Vaughan had left the pickup unlocked. Downey sneaked past and stuck the manila envelope on the floor under the front seat, the first place a cop looks when he is searching a vehicle.

They left DeLuca in Miami. Greco didn't expect a man like DeLuca to involve himself on the point-and-shoot level, but considering that they were strangers in town, it would have been helpful to come along and make sure they were going the right way on the Interstate. The arrows got confusing as hell out by the airport, and Greco wasted an hour before he could get himself straightened out. Nick slept through it all. He was in a terrible mood when he woke up, depressed and paranoid, and Greco had to give him a real locker-room talk—don't let your friends down, so on and so forth—and tell him how easy it was going to be. It had to be easy, in fact, or they would go back to the girls, and tell DeLuca they hadn't been able to find the fat man.

According to DeLuca, Canada had been kidnapped, not by professionals who knew what they were doing, but by a couple of two-bit boppers. Their target would be immobilized, without bodyguards, pinpointed, an easy knock-over. It would seem that the kidnappers had killed him, and there would be less heat. Canada's loyal followers wouldn't be thinking in terms of revenge, and the transition would go smoothly. There would be rumors that DeLuca had masterminded it, but that was O.K. It would show he was capable of using his head. If he saw a chance of avoiding trouble for himself and his people, he took it.

Greco was used to parking lots, but this one, plunked down in the middle of unfriendly countryside, was ridiculous. He thought at first it was going to be like looking for one particular car at Shea Stadium during a Mets double-header, in short, impossible. They were looking for a white pickup with a camper body over the cab. It turned out that there weren't too many of those. They drove up and down the streets until they found it. Now what to do? As far as he could tell, only one road connected the parked trailers with the highway. That could be blocked by a single car. Whenever Greco went into a restaurant, he looked around for the exits before sitting down because he wanted to have a choice of directions. He decided there was only one thing to do here—leave the car on the highway and walk in. He drove back, found a grassy place where he could pull over, then raised the hood when he left, to indicate engine trouble in case anyone wondered.

Nick didn't like it. His platform shoes were designed for walking across carpets, not ground. Greco explained it: if they got caught in there, with their car on the wrong side of a barricade, they were in trouble. There were no subway stations in this part of the world. They needed wheels.

Nick continued to grumble. He tried walking in stocking feet. That wasn't much better. Strange noises came from the vegetation. He was hobbling badly by the time they came in. Greco immediately saw one defect in his plan. In here, nobody walked. On their own two feet, they stood out, especially in their Miami Beach clothes. So he picked up a gas can from beside one of the dark trailers. Now if anybody saw them, they were going for gas.

"I didn't think it would be like this," Nick complained.

Neither had Greco. Having lived his whole life in a city, he would have preferred a city location. To date, he had killed two people. The first time, he had been angry. The guy had lied to him and tricked him, and he deserved what he got. Greco was surprised at how little it affected him. He had thought it would be more of a high. The next time, he was driven to a bar in the South Bronx. His man didn't know him, but he saw something in Greco's manner. He had a reddish face, with a little map of the circulatory system on his cheeks, and in one second he turned as white as a piece of paper. He shrank back, holding up one hand. That had been nice.

Now, if he did well on this, it could lead to something else. The word gets around: Greco isn't only a short-range bar shooter, he's a boy who can hit the good curve. Anybody could do that Bronx job. But to go after somebody in a strange environment with an inexperienced partner, come through, and get away clean, for that kind of out-of-the-ordinary thing you can name your own price.

"You've still got the gun."

"Mother of God," Nick exclaimed, clapping his

stomach. Then he gave his goofy laugh. "Sure I got it. Stop pissing your pants."

It was his first joke in an hour, which meant he was feeling better. Greco was sharp and ready. Simpson, the scared junky, had said there were two vehicles parked separately, the trailer with the stolen stuff in it and their own pickup. A gun to their head. "Where's the fucking trailer?" No point in a massacre; tie the jerks up after they told him would be good enough. Then Canada. Strangulation would be quieter, neater.

At the pickup camper, he whispered directions to Nick. They took out their guns. But out of the corner of his eye, he saw a police car blinking its way in from the highway. It couldn't have anything to do with them, Greco and Nick, because as far as they were concerned they hadn't done anything yet.

"What's the matter, what's the matter?" Nick whispered.

One more difference between a trailer park and an ordinary parking lot is that most of the vehicles are too tall to see over. The police car came on, appearing and disappearing. When it turned into their street, Greco hit Nick on the shoulder, and they got down out of sight, wriggling well in. It was a trailer on blocks, far enough off the ground so Greco didn't think they would get too much oil on their clothes.

The patrol car stopped beside the Benjamin-Vaughan pickup, and the cops came boiling out.

"Shake it down," a voice said.

The two guys inside were awakened roughly and made to step out while the truck was searched. When something was found under the front seat, the cops were extremely pleased, the guys were surprised and indignant. A search warrant was mentioned. The cops had one, as it happened, for precisely this pickup, with the right marker number. It was a dope thing, as far as Greco could figure. There was a lot of loud talk. Lights went on, and the people in the trailer above them began moving around. Greco put a hand on the small of Nick's back to keep him from shaking and transmitting his shakes to the trailer floor. One of the cops crawled part way under the pickup with a flashlight. Greco and Nick, only one vehicle away, lay absolutely still, hoping to be mistaken for unevenness in the ground.

It was over finally, and the area began to settle down. Above them, the man wanted some sex before he went back to sleep. The woman didn't, and she prevailed. The quarrel was clearly audible through the floor. Time went slowly for the two New Yorkers. Was there anything they could do now but go home? They couldn't break into every unattached trailer on the grounds, looking for the one that held Canada. De-Luca would understand that.

Still, Greco wasn't quite ready to give up. When the guys said they'd never seen that envelope, it had sounded sincere. And if they were out robbing in Homestead, they couldn't be down in Key West picking up shit, could they? So if somebody wanted them out of the way, it would have been easy to walk by and drop an envelope in the truck. It would do no harm to stick around a few minutes and find out.

Nick had to piss. Greco told him, for God's sake, to roll over and piss. The stream was cut off abruptly as footsteps approached.

Two men and a woman stopped beside the pickup. One of the men said, "There's a handle on the hitch jack. When the ball and the socket come together, you snap the top half over and hook on the chains. Snap in the electric. I want to do it in one pass if I can, get out of here fast."

The woman said nervously, "Are you really sure Canada is in there? I think we ought to check, break in."

"Too many people still awake. Didn't I see him? If that wasn't Canada, what was he doing tied to the bed?"

"Laundry or something?" the other male voice suggested.

"I saw him *breathing*, I tell you."

Chapter 12

Inside the baited trailer, Shayne heard a truck go by, brake, and come back. Frieda was sleeping. She awakened instantly at his touch.

The driver of the pickup either had a good eye or he was getting good directions; he made the hitch in one move. Somebody spoke sharply. It sounded to Shayne like the voice that had shouted commands at Canada over the bullhorn.

Frieda was on her feet, the gun in her hand. "Take them now?" she whispered.

Shayne shook his head. This time he was armed, but he wanted if possible to do it without shooting. There were too many people sleeping around them. Rourke would follow when they moved out. If they were too badly outnumbered, he could call for help on the van's phone.

They got away with a jerk. The wide road had been ditched with a succession of shallow speed bumps. They took the first of these too fast, and the jolt caused the big payloader tire to waver out from the wall. Shayne wedged it back. On his first inspection, he had noticed a two-way phone system in the little kitchen. Usually these things were designed so only one end had a talk button. The other end never stopped transmitting. Using his flashlight, he found the instrument and turned up the volume.

"Stop bitching," a voice said, and another voice answered, too faint to be heard.

The first voice: "Oh, that went beautiful. Smooth as silk. Show these country slobs a couple of ounces of real H and they go out of their skulls. A little confusion right now is all to the good. Muddy the waters, you know? The thing of it is, we're completely anonymous."

"I'll sell you my share right now for sixty thousand."

"If I had sixty thousand, I'd take you up on that, boy. I think Larry would like to set a record, don't you? Help the image. All this extra trouble, we ought to revise the numbers. How does a million and a quarter sound?" After a moment: "Well, hell, a straight million. It's easier to take in."

"*Will everybody please keep quiet for a minute?*"

It was a woman's voice.

The long wait under the trailer had made Greco sluggish. They had to be back in their rented car by the time the pickup and the thieves' trailer pulled out of the park. He was trying to think ahead to their next move.

And then he had a truly sensational idea, the best idea so far. Explosion and fire! Earlier he had ripped off somebody's gas can to have something to carry. Now he ran back to get it. Nick wanted to know what he was doing.

"Tell you in a minute."

Pam, sitting between the two men in the cab of the pickup, had a different kind of pressure coming at her from opposite sides. That strength and certainty of Downey's, she was beginning to see, masked a kind of obtuseness. What made people take the police exam in the first place? Whatever it was, Downey had it in excess. In that threesome, he was the man of experience. When he spoke, everything about his tone and manner declared that he knew what he was talking about. Events frequently proved that he didn't. It never fazed him a bit. His ego was iron-bound. He wanted more than compliance, he wanted admiration.

As he drove, his hand dropped to its usual place on the inside of her thigh. Perhaps he had forgotten Werner. Perhaps this was merely an announcement of how things were going to be from then on. It was impossible to tell what Werner was thinking.

Downey had decided to drive to the truck stop where they had left Werner's car, and put Canada into that for the rest of the journey. It wouldn't be easy, maneuvering that dead weight between vehicles, but when they got to Miami Heights they could off-load in the garage with the door down. The trailer wouldn't be seen entering their driveway. They could sort out the cars afterward.

The great field was between crops at the moment. A certain amount of vegetable litter had been left lying around, but absolutely nothing was growing in the poisoned soil. Nick was carrying his shoes. They moved at a pace between a walk and a shambling run. There had been clouds earlier. Now there were stars, and it seemed to Greco that whenever he looked up he saw a meteor. On the way in, they had aimed at the lights of the camp. Now there was nothing but stars, and even they didn't seem to want to hold still.

Nick was swearing a steady stream. Every time he stepped on something sharp, he hated Greco more. He thought it had been stupid to leave the car so far away. That trailer would haul-ass out in a minute, and if they weren't in their own car by then, they couldn't hope to overtake it. It was Greco's fault, but they would both be blamed.

"DeLuca won't listen to alibis. He'll cut off our balls."

"Or give us a medal, one."

The gas can kept banging against Greco's leg, and he was tempted to throw it away. But he hung onto it. They still had a way to go when the pickup and trailer combination came under the lighted sign.

"We won't make it," Nick gasped.

"Oh, yes, we will," Greco said grimly.

Taking his partner's arm, he ran with him until they went out of step and he had to let go. But the ground was smoother here, and all of a sudden they were on the road. The pickup began its turn, and Greco pulled Nick down so they wouldn't be seen in the headlights. Another undignified move, and Greco, with his mouth full of dirt, was hoping it might be the last.

He ran ahead, slammed the lifted hood of the car, and was back on pavement by the time Nick hobbled up. The trailer's hind end, lit up like a Macy's window, dwindled away. Another camping vehicle, this one a van—a Dodge, Greco thought—came out of the park.

"What are we getting into here, a shoot-out?" Nick demanded. "Three people is already too many."

"Hell with them," Greco said, having to smile. "No shooting. We're going to set the mother on fire."

"How, throw matches?"

"Why do you think I lugged this Goddamn can? There's gas sloshing around in there."

Dazed as he was, Nick took a moment to see it. "You mean give them a cocktail."

"That's just what I mean. They won't even know what happened. DeLuca will love it."

He was shifting up fast, getting all the acceleration out of the car that it was willing to give them. They had a bottle of rum in the back seat. Nick pissed it out the window as they went. When the bottle was empty, he gave Greco a nod. Greco stopped to let him pour. Without a funnel, he spilled quite a bit. When Greco was unable to find a rag, Nick contributed a sock, which he soaked in gas and twisted up tight to make a wick.

Shayne, in the kitchen of the moving trailer, listened closely to the conversation in the cab. The driver continued to boast of how well he had read the scene at the hot plant. He was the one who had insisted they shouldn't give up. And did they know why? Because he knew the criminal mentality.

The woman was needling him more and more openly. He wasn't getting it yet.

"Mike."

Frieda gestured urgently from the doorway. Shayne jumped to join her.

She had tilted the slats when she looked to be sure

that Rourke, in the van, had followed them out. The van was an eighth of a mile back, ambling along at a comfortable forty-five, the minimum on this road. Now Shayne saw a black sedan beginning to pull out to pass them.

Frieda whispered, "They came up before and dropped back. Two men. Something peculiar about them."

Shayne caught the license number as the car crept closer. It was a rented Ford from the Hertz fleet. The driver, young and dark, was clutching the wheel as though about to go into a dangerous skidding turn, although the highway here ran as straight as a ruled line. The man beside him was fiddling with something on his lap.

These couldn't be cops. Canada's men wouldn't be driving a rented car. Nevertheless, it seemed to Shayne that a strange electricity was flickering in that front seat. His eye jumped to his .367. It was across the trailer, where they had arranged the lamps so their beams would converge on the door.

For an instant, the second man in the Ford looked straight at the trailer window. His face was in eruption. His head bobbed at the end of a stalklike neck. His hands came up, and when Shayne saw the flame of a cigarette lighter, he came around fast. There was no time for the gun. He kicked a chair aside and dislodged the great payloader wheel. It started to move, and Shayne gave it a hard push as it passed. It came up hard against the back wall. The sudden weight shift caused the trailer to veer toward the Ford.

The two windows were almost parallel when it happened, the window at Nick's elbow and the trailer's window. Greco was riding the brake, giving him plenty of time. It was an easy side-hand toss, but it had to shatter the glass and get through the blind.

With a faint clash of metal, the vehicles kissed. Greco had seen the fishtail starting and instinctively twitched away. It was this more than the slight collision that threw Nick off. He couldn't wait to make sure that the flame had taken hold. He had to touch it off and throw in the same motion, and he couldn't afford to miss. If he missed and the flaming gas dribbled harmlessly onto the highway, Canada's kidnappers would know they were under attack, and out would come the guns. Greco would have to pull alongside, and it would be Nick who would bear the brunt of the shooting. Three people, three guns, and nowadays women could shoot, too, you know.

When the trailer's bumper dug into their rear door panel, crumpling it inward, the throw was already underway. Nick started back in horror as a ball of fire exploded directly in front of his eyes.

The bottle had shattered on the edge of the window frame, breaking a pane and sending some of the blazing fluid into the trailer. But much of the explosion came back into the Ford. Nick yelled in astonishment, swinging his arms like a man attacked by hornets.

"Stop! Stop!"

Greco was fighting the wheel. He swerved back across both lanes and finally brought the car to a shuddering stop in the dirt.

Nick fell out, uttering sharp, high-pitched screams. His loose shirt was on fire. He whipped it over his head, setting fire to his hair. Greco embraced him roughly and put out the flames with his hands.

Nick's thin screams subsided to moans. "It hurts, Greco, it hurts."

Greco's hands were hurting, too, but that didn't

mean they could stand there feeling sorry for themselves. Their good plan had gone sour for reasons Greco was unable to understand. That trailer had behaved as though King Kong or somebody had given it a push. It was already out of sight down the road. The gas Nick had slopped around when he was filling the bottle had caught fire with a whoosh, and the Ford's front-seat compartment was burning fiercely. Greco backed away. This was a fire nobody would put out with his hands.

Headlights were coming toward them. It was the same Dodge van he had seen coming out of the trailer park. When Greco saw that they didn't intend to stop, he leaped out, waving both arms and yelling.

The van swung to the right, trying to get by on the inside. Greco snatched out his gun and popped a shot through the windshield. It was done without aiming, but he aimed the next one, and when the driver realized what Greco was aiming at, and at that range was unlikely to miss, he put on his brakes and came skidding up to within a couple of feet of the blazing Ford.

Greco was so mad at this guy for his lack of concern for a fellow motorist in trouble that he was ready to shoot him out if he didn't get out of his own free will. He must have conveyed that purpose, and the driver, a tall skinny fellow in glasses, slid to the ground, vibrating.

"What the hell is the gun for? I'll drive you."

"Get over there," Greco snarled.

Doing what the gun told him, the thin man moved out in the weeds. Greco yelled for Nick, who was standing on the roadside, not in too great shape. Another yell brought him out of it. He looked for his gun. It was probably still in the burning car. Greco really yelled the next time, and Nick started toward him. They needed both guns, but the way Greco felt now, he was willing to take on the whole outfit with only his teeth and his fingernails.

Chapter 13

The curtains blazed up. The gas had splashed as far as the opposite wall. The stolen equipment from the construction site, along with everything else, had been tumbled about by the collision. There had to be a fire extinguisher somewhere, but there was no time to find it.

The great tire blocked them off from the worst corner, and it was firmly lodged. The wall-to-wall carpet would be the worst problem. Frieda was wielding a heavy drape. The fire retreated after each swing, but instantly recovered. The sofa caught. Now they were blocked from the door.

As long as they continued to move at the same speed, they could hold the fire in this room. The instant they stopped, the whole thing would go up. Using the butt of his pistol, Shayne hammered the glass out of the bedroom window beside the pillows he had arranged to look like an unconscious man. Then he punched the talk button on the two-way phone.

"Your trailer's on fire. Pull over."

He knew at once from the deadness of the sound that the trailer's swing had snapped the connection. There had to be some way to get the attention of the people in the cab. If he and Frieda came through opposite windows at the same time, they still might be able to make the capture.

He was looking for something to throw. The first thing he considered was the oxygen tank of a welding outfit. Another possibility hit him. He remembered throwing a torch into the payloader bucket. If he could find that, he could cut their way out and climb through into the pickup.

Frieda was pushing furniture into the fire, trying to make a firebreak. It wasn't working.

"Hold it three minutes?" Shayne shouted.

"Try."

He spotted the torch. He found the acetylene and made his connections in a hurry. Pushing too hard, he broke his last match. He tore a page from a cookbook, twisted it into a long spill, and lit it at the fire. In another moment, the torch was spitting. He adjusted the mixture, modulating the flame from orange to a hot, hard blue.

Kicking everything out of his way, he began work on the wall. The flame went through the thin sheet metal like a knife through ice cream, leaving a charred line from floor to ceiling. Frieda retreated down the passageway, using her drape as a flail, while he completed a crude door. As the cuts joined, the metal section fell inward.

"Frieda."

She had lost her cap. Her hair had come loose, and her face was smeared with soot. She looked marvelous, as always.

Holding on with one hand, he reached across to the pickup and opened the back door. He stayed there, straddling the gap, while Frieda squeezed past. A sudden change of direction would have spilled them both on the highway, but the engineers who designed the highway had believed that the straightest road is the shortest and fastest and therefore the best. Flames filled the kitchen and one bedroom. Frieda shifted her grip from the jagged metal edge to Shayne's shoulder, then to the roof of the pickup, and swung on in.

Shayne followed her across. Their speed had dropped to thirty and was still dropping. Perhaps the driver had realized finally that something unusual was taking place behind him.

Shayne crouched to disengage the hitch. He unhooked the chains and snapped the latch. The ball still rode snugly in its socket. Getting a good grip, he jumped hard on the bumper, and the burning trailer pulled free.

They would be changing vehicles in another ten miles. When Downey saw the headlights closing with him—an ordinary black Ford or Chevy, nothing to worry about, except that, being in charge, he was the one who had to worry about everything—he picked the dark glasses off his knee. He had killed the dashboard lights earlier. Pam was about to start a cigarette. He told her to wait till the car was past.

"In fact," he said, watching the mirror, "get down on the floor. A pickup and trailer, two men and a girl. You never know, they might just remember."

Pam slid to the floor and tugged at Werner's pants until he followed, with a sigh of protest. The headlights came closer, much too slowly. Downey decided to brake as soon as they were alongside, timing it so they wouldn't notice his brake lights, and let them scoot past. But it was the other car that braked and fell back.

Pam, on the floor, could tell something was wrong. "Jack?"

"Somebody wants to play games."

The overhead mirror was blocked by the camper body. He was driving with the two big side mirrors. Their lights stayed in his eyes.

"Creeping paranoia," Werner remarked. "Poor Jack, everybody's chasing him."

"If they want to pass, why don't they pass? We're only doing forty-five. Here that's crawling."

The lights came at him again even more slowly. Downey had an impulse to hog the center line until the next exit, and if they followed him off, he would know they were hostile. But with that enormous trailer behind him, he had to play it conservative. He wasn't used to driving this much vehicle. He felt slow and unwieldy, like a pro basketball center in a room with ordinary people.

He glanced at the speedometer, wanting to see what they did if he dropped his road speed again. He felt a distinct jar, and his eyes jumped to the mirror.

"He cut in on me!"

The trailer was swinging. It swung away, back, away again.

"They're on fire!"

The car behind them drifted out on the shoulder, definitely burning. Flames showed through the windshield. The others scrambled back on the seat, and Werner put his head out the window.

"What happened?" Pam said in the middle. "Tell me what happened."

The burning car pulled over, and two figures jumped out, one of them ablaze. Downey came down on the gas. He wasn't about to back up and help. Let the fuckers burn. Some kind of freak accident that couldn't happen again in a hundred years. Brakes probably. They were driving with their emergency on, which was why the car had seemed slow to respond. When flames came up through the floorboards, the driver had been so startled that he jerked over and rammed Downey's trailer. Drunk? Undoubtedly.

Werner said, "Man, they're burning."

"That's their problem. How about our back lights? Are they on?"

Werner craned all the way out. "No," he reported. "So if we pass a cop, we can expect to hear sirens."

"Not for the first time tonight," Pam put in.

"Nobody cruises this late," Downey told them. "We're going to do the last stretch on a side road, if I can get that son of a bitch to start tracking."

He maintained a hard foot on the gas, but the trailer continued to wander. He was getting a bumping, an irregular oscillation. Perhaps the jolt had broken something loose, and it was rolling around in there. He could still see the glow from the burning car, and he decided against stopping until they had left the four-lane. The next exit was a quarter of a mile ahead, then presently an eighth of a mile. He shifted down for the ramp.

Suddenly his front wheels bucked, as though they had struck a speed bump like those in the trailer camp. But on the *Interstate*? He continued the turn, and the feel of everything changed. They were no longer pulling a load.

The ramp curved away. Without quite believing it, he saw their unattached trailer, still on the main highway, continuing south. And it, too, was on fire!

That was the worst thing yet on a bad night. Some supernatural force must be working against them. Downey straightened the wheel in time to keep from leaving the ramp. The pickup was enjoying its freedom.

"There goes our million bucks," Werner observed.

What was he talking about? The only million-dollar object around here—and then it came to him. A vise seemed to close on his head. Canada was inside that trailer, tied to a bed.

The trailer continued to pick up speed, coming down from the overpass. It was beginning to drift. Soon its outside wheels were off on the shoulder. It ran down a slight embankment, hit the fence, and kept going into a cultivated field. A million dollars. No chance of getting anybody out of that fire. It was out of control.

Pam clawed at his shoulder and pointed. He saw it, a big irrigation wagon standing all by itself well out in the field. He understood what she was shouting. But the way their luck seemed to be running, the wagon had to be empty. If there was water in it, there was no way to bring it to bear on the fire.

The trailer changed direction, moving less rapidly on the uneven ground, and headed straight for the water wagon like a camel smelling a well.

Downey cut so hard that he jumped the ramp at the bottom. The fence protected only the ramps and the big highway itself. He went straight in across country, dropping into the pickup's bottom range. The field was in snap beans, nearly ready for the pickers. His rear wheels kicked out torn plants and soft dirt.

The trailer stayed upright, stopping only fifty feet from the wagon. He dropped Werner, who ran ahead. Downey came swerving in and stopped with the trailer in his lights. Inside, the fire was crackling nicely, but it was giving off little heat. He was able to get almost to the bedroom window, through which earlier he had seen the kidnapped man on the bed. This was the one room not ablaze. There still might be time.

He heard a yell from Werner. Turning, he saw a plume of water erupt from the tank and start a long sweep to the right and the left. Downey felt mist blow in his face. The main arc, however, was missing the trailer by twenty feet. Werner struggled with the short hose on the turret's fixed arm. He managed to free it. It lashed around madly, spraying everything at random. He worked his hands toward the nozzle, brought it under control, and aimed the powerful stream at the fire. Perhaps by accident, he caught Downey in the chest and knocked him to the ground. Correcting his aim, he sent a cascade of water through the bedroom window.

The van Greco had appropriated proved to be unexpectedly agile. The brakes were so good that when he touched them lightly to get the feel the sudden check nearly sent him into the glass.

"This baby has power."

The needle hit seventy in no time at all. Nick was worrying about what they would do when they overtook the trailer. They couldn't attempt the same trick a second time because the gas can was empty.

"Bottle gas," Greco said. "These things carry stoves. Look in back."

"Bottle gas! That stuff can blow your ass off. I'll drive this time. You throw."

"No, *it worked, it worked*! Burning like a son of a bitch."

In the fields to the right, they saw the burning trailer. So, after all, some of the improvised cocktail had taken effect. Greco stopped so they could watch the finish.

There was a noise in back, and somebody groaned. They looked at each other.

"We got company," Greco said.

Then water jetted up out of a standing wagon and began to fall on the flames. The smoke changed color. Another minute or two and the fire would be out. They would transfer Canada to the pickup and be on their way. An attack on that crowd with only one gun was out of the question.

"Up and down all night," Nick said. "Up and down. Let's go back to the hotel."

"No, listen, if we can keep them back from the fire—"

And he was out and running. He went through the break in the fence, going flat on his face after five steps. He saw two figures near the trailer, one more on the wagon. He brought out the gun. All he had to do was knock the man off the wagon, then pop off a shot or two to persuade the others to keep their heads down. The fire would take hold again, and soon nothing would be left of Canada but bones and charred flesh.

He was breathing hard from the run, and he couldn't get the sights to hold steady. He fired anyway. The bullet hit the tank and went singing away, going nowhere. The guy dropped to the ground, but the nozzle was wedged in place, and water continued to splash into the trailer. Maybe Canada would swallow enough smoke so he wouldn't wake up. Maybe not, too. It would be so nice to make sure.

Then he saw Nick running in a wide circle, heading for the wagon. Greco had to revise his opinion of the boy. He had been nothing but a drag so far, clowning when he wasn't complaining, and then finally losing his gun. But even to think about climbing on that wagon, that took balls.

He came up on one knee. The minute Nick started his climb, he intended to waste a couple just for the hell of it. All Nick had to do was give the nozzle one swipe and then slide to the ground. In movies, people did things like that all the time.

And there the prick was, edging along the top of the tank. Greco kept swiveling, watching for movement. Sure enough, a head came up, but in an unexpected place. The guy had fooled him by wriggling between the bean rows. He fired at Nick, Nick fell forward against the nozzle. The stream's force flung him off the tank, leaving the nozzle whipping about like something alive. At the trailer, flames appeared again almost at once amid the masses of smoke.

Everybody was out of sight again, and Greco dropped out of sight also. Now he would find out if any of those jokers was man enough to climb up the way Nick had done and redirect the hose. Greco was closer now, and he was feeling the heat. This was one shot he didn't intend to miss.

The trailer was burning from one end to the other. Larry Canada was done for, and Greco and Nick could collect their money. Abruptly the hose stopped lashing around and hung down lankly, with only a dribble coming out. And then there was an immense bang from the trailer, sending a column of sparks and flame hundreds of feet in the air.

Chapter 14

The search for contraband drugs at the trailer park had left the interior of the pickup a tangled mess. The beds had been pulled apart. When the brakes went on hard, Shayne was thrown to the floor.

"There goes our million bucks," a voice said in the cab.

The woman shouted something, and the pickup began bucking and plunging. It came to a stop, and everybody piled out, Shayne and Frieda moving more cautiously than the three in front. Shayne saw the burning trailer, the three running figures. In a moment, a new grouping took shape, and water began to fall on the fire.

"How are we going to do this?" Frieda said.

"Wait for Tim. We can pin them down here until he gets us some cops."

On the highway, the big van slowed to a stop. Shayne blinked his flashlight twice, shielding the beam. A figure appeared, as though in response to the signal.

"It's not Tim," Frieda said.

Shayne looked around quickly. Whoever Frieda had seen had dropped out of sight.

Here was a new factor, and until Shayne could see how it fitted in, they would have to watch the action without taking part. They moved back from the truck. He heard a stealthy, animal-like movement behind him, and a figure passed within a few feet. It was the youth who had thrown the bomb. Now he was bare from the waist up—stick-figure arms, shoulder blades that stuck out like cleavers. There were two sides here, and both sides must believe Larry Canada was a prisoner in the trailer. Beyond that, Shayne had to wait and see.

The fire had almost been brought under control when the bare-chested youth climbed onto the wagon and took a shot in the stomach, dislodging the hose as he fell. A moment later the trailer was blazing again. The tire exploded, blowing out several of the riveted panels. The entire interior was now one mass of flame.

Shayne heard a stifled exclamation from Frieda. The van on the highway was beginning to move.

"Somebody's driving off with our fat man," she said.

"Let's go get them."

They returned to the truck. He let out the clutch the instant the motor took hold, and they shot forward. He felt a wash of heat as they passed the fire. Somebody jumped aside. He had a gun in his hand, and so did Frieda. Neither one fired.

Downey, his hand raised against the heat, backed away. He saw the pickup start for the gap in the fence and yelled to Pam, "Werner—the son of a bitch is taking off. We should have got rid of that bastard when we had the chance."

Then Werner himself came running past. He gave Downey a look with murder in it and disappeared in the darkness. That might be a good example for everybody to follow. The fire trucks would be showing up any minute now.

Pam was still on her knees, looking pale and sick. To bring her out of it, Downey flicked the side of her face with his fingers as he went past. "Let's go, let's go."

The damn place was as bright as day. He had counted two people. Two vehicles had driven off. But suddenly he was convinced that there was someone he hadn't counted, a marksman, who even now was aiming a high-velocity rifle at his spinal column. He felt conspicuous and fragile. He broke stride and dodged about in the beans like a running back.

Then he was in the shadow cast by the water wagon. He ran along that. He was out of condition for this, and after a time he had to drop to the ground to wait for his breath to come back.

The highway was empty now, but that couldn't continue long. The van and the pickup had passed out of sight. Who the hell *were* those guys? He would have said Benjamin and Vaughan, but that pair was locked away for the night. He just didn't know anymore. He got a certain arrangement in the kaleidoscope, and then somebody bumped his elbow and everything came out different.

The trailer was burning like a beacon, with the flames standing straight up. Pam and Werner were nowhere. Downey was alone in the vast field—no friends, no transportation. He had only a vague idea of the geography around here. When he went anywhere, he went on paved roads. He decided to return to the county road that passed under the Interstate, and follow that to see where it led. He trudged off, beginning to wonder if it wouldn't have been better to try and live on the pension.

He heard Pam and Werner snapping at each other ahead and ran to catch up, glad to know he wouldn't be alone on the walk. He neglected to call out who he was, and they went headlong.

"It's Jack!" he announced.

He heard the click of a hammer coming back, a scary sound anywhere, and he did another complicated dive and roll. He drew his own gun.

"Hey, let's not split up. We can still pull this off. Maybe not the full million, but hell, let's get our expenses out, anyway."

He went on talking as he crawled. He had really given up back there when he realized that Canada was being fried in his own deep fat. He was only talking to ground some of the electricity in the air. But he began to see possibilities, and by the time he reached them, he had nearly convinced himself.

"You're still thinking about money?" Pam said with scorn. "Jack, you're insane."

"A better word would be stubborn," Downey said. "Everybody knows that about me. Once I take hold of a thing, I never let go."

"We're all still alive. That's more than can be said for some people. Let's go our separate ways."

"Can't do that yet," Downey said plausibly. "We're going to be traveling in the same car. Werner, how's the arm?"

"I'm O.K."

"I thought I'd suggest, as soon as we hit a road, why don't we find you a place to sit down, and we'll go get the car and come back for you? No sense in us all walking."

"I don't want to feel left out."

"Suit yourself."

Werner had pocketed his gun, but he kept his hand in that pocket. Downey did the same, until he persuaded himself that everything was cool. Reaching the road, they turned east. Sooner or later they would be bound to see signs.

"Now why should anybody want to set that trailer on fire?" he said. "Because they knew Canada was in it! Are you following me this far? He's stepped on so many faces, the town's full of people who'd like to see him burn."

They were listening, at least. If he was this tired at the start, how would he feel at the finish? They could droop along and admit that their feet hurt. But he was the noncom, he had to pretend.

"We could go home and get some sleep," he said, "and by the time we woke up, everything would be buttoned up tight. Damn it, this was a great idea of yours, Werner. I for one don't want to give up just because we had a little setback here."

"A little setback," Werner repeated in an amazed voice.

"Not so little, I guess. Here's what I was thinking. We've got the letter ready. Let's go ahead and send the fucking thing. When the wife gets it, she'll call a committee meeting. One man on that committee is going to know there's no point, because Canada is out on the Interstate in a burnt-out trailer. But he can't say so without giving it away. They'll go ahead and collect the money—"

"First making sure he's alive," Pam said.

"That's where you're wrong. With a number that big, they won't *deliver* the money until they're sure he's alive, but they'll collect it. They'll have it on hand. One million cash. Now they're disorganized. Their security won't be of the best. Do you see what I'm driving at? It's a police matter. I'll be in on it. I'll see how they act, and I'll keep in touch with you guys so you can move on a minute's notice. Who the hell knows? Maybe I'll give you a call and tell you to put on the masks. We won't go for the guy this time, go for the money."

He was forcing it. He didn't believe himself it would happen. Enough was enough.

He had guessed about ten miles. It was more like fifteen. Dawn was about due by the time they sighted the car. Several times, approaching headlights had made them dive for the side of the road. Toward the end, they were hopelessly lost. He couldn't keep talking the whole time, but he thought he finally convinced Pam. Werner, probably not. He had to keep an eye on that boy.

"Nick, Nick." Greco pulled him out from under the water wagon and came down beside him. "You're a mess, you know that?"

Greco had to feel an effect from the way Nick was looking at him. It was touching. Nick had gathered some bean plants and was pressing them to the wound. It was no substitute for regular bandages. If Greco attempted to carry him, he was going to get blood and slime all over his clothes. Nick's acne stood out as though it had been stippled on. The medal on his chest winked in the firelight.

He tried to make it a real smile. "Think I broke the ankle."

Greco looked. A foot usually sticks out in the shape of an L. This was more of a W.

"Uh-oh. You won't do any walking on that."

"I took care of their Goddamn water for them, didn't I?"

"Nick, the way you skinned up on that thing—"

Indeed, thanks to Nick's exploit, they had accomplished what they had set out to accomplish. Greco felt a pulse of affection for the goofy kid. Nothing faggish about it, it was more of an army thing, one soldier to another. That didn't help with the main problem. The nearest hospital was Miami, and they sure as hell were in no condition to hitchhike. How would they answer the questions when they got there?

The soggy mass on Nick's stomach shifted, and if Greco's own stomach hadn't been somewhat uneasy by now, he could have looked inside and seen what his friend had eaten for supper. Nick was getting paler by the second. Greco could see he would have to do all the work. He folded the limp body into sitting position and tried to lift. It was too slippery. Nick was unable to give him any help at all.

Greco was casting about for some marvelous solution. He couldn't come up with one. It would be hard enough to get out of this himself without being held back by a gut-shot cripple who from the look of it was going to die anyway. Even if he had an ambulance waiting, which he didn't, Nick would be out of the picture before they were halfway. And leaving him here wouldn't be much better. They'd get his fingerprints and check the hotels. They'd signed in at the Doral under their right names, which had probably been dumb. DeLuca? He wouldn't even help with the lawyer.

He smelled Nick's burned hair, and that gave him the idea. He had somehow managed to hoist his friend up on his one good ankle. Nick was already close to collapse, and they hadn't gone anywhere yet. He tried to get his weight distributed properly, but Greco thought, why bother?

The two had gone to the same high school. Greco let Nick tag along on a couple of small deals. He sponsored him, in a way. Nick had a brother who dealt, and he could always get whatever he wanted for parties. They'd been having such a great time in Miami.

"Have ourselves a ball with that money," Nick said feebly when Greco stopped to get a less slippery grip. "Mexico—" Trying to smile, he said it again like the Mexicans. "Meh-hico."

True, there had been some stoned talk about taking the girls to Mexico City after DeLuca paid them off. It wouldn't happen now. Greco started moving again, and when Nick understood, he whimpered in disbelief. Greco ran him straight at the fire. It was too hot to go all the way. About four feet from one of the sprung panels, he dug in and let go, giving Nick a hard final push combined with a lift.

It was a terrible look that Nick gave Greco, and at the last moment he was screaming. He went inside in a shower of sparks. Greco would remember that look and that scream, but it was just something he would have to learn to live with. He was doing his friend a favor, as well as himself, getting it over in an instant instead of leaving him to die slowly in pain.

A car was slowing on the highway. Greco ran toward it, and when he got within negotiating distance, he took out his gun. He must have been fairly wild-looking by now. There were two people inside, a kid at the wheel and the thin, jangly looking man Greco had forced out of the Dodge van. He waved his weapon, and they both got out.

"Not again," the thin man said. "What happened to everybody?"

Greco couldn't have answered that question even if he had wanted to. As soon as the car was empty, he jumped in and took off.

Chapter 15

The van was moving erratically between lanes. Shayne, in the pickup camper, closed with it rapidly, flicking his headlights. With a competent driver and its initial advantage, the van could have outrun them, but whoever was at the wheel was having all he could do to stay on the highway. As Shayne came into position, he saw that it wasn't somebody hijacking Canada, it was Canada himself.

He overflowed onto the steering wheel. He gave them a dazed look. Frieda nodded pleasantly and showed him the gun.

His mouth opened, and he stamped on the gas. Shayne was a half-length ahead now. He bore in sharply and herded the van off the asphalt. The fat man finally went to his brake. He stopped well off the road.

Frieda descended, the gun still out. Shayne pulled past and parked. Canada recognized him when he came into the headlights.

"Mike Shayne. Am I glad to see you! I thought—"

"We'll talk in a minute, Larry. If we stay here, we'll collect a crowd."

"Do you know what happened? They jumped me, they chloroformed me—"

"They?" Shayne said coldly. "What do you think this is, a rescue?"

Canada looked uneasily from Shayne to Frieda, and to the gun in Frieda's hand. "You aren't going to try to tell me—"

"Get in back and shut up."

Canada's jaw fell open. "You mean that was you in those masks? I don't believe it."

Shayne clicked his fingernail against the door. "Move, Larry."

Canada had difficulty freeing himself. He side-stepped between the seats. Frieda came in back with him, returning the gun to her shoulder bag. Canada made a hard landing on one of the beds, looking mis-understood and confused. His white suit had been disheveled to start with, and it had deteriorated badly in the last several hours while he was moved from his smashed Cadillac to the sand pile and on into the van. He licked his full lips.

"You wouldn't have anything to eat, would you?"

"Later," Shayne said from the wheel.

He crossed the median and headed back toward the fire. Three cars had stopped. Rourke saw him, walked away from the group casually, and crossed the high-way.

"You had me worried," he said, coming in. "Then I saw the place where you cut your way out. That's a good rule. Never get trapped in a burning trailer without the right tools. How are you, Larry?"

"You're in on this, too?"

"You're my project for the month. Maybe we ought to get moving, Mike."

"No, I want Larry to see it. Struggle up, Larry."

Canada forced himself out from the wall, and Frieda parted the curtains.

"All right. A trailer. It's on fire. So?"

"The people who set it on fire thought you were in it."

He saw a flashing light coming fast and went into gear. The cops were only interested in what was happening on the southbound lanes. They would find one burned-out Ford, one trailer still burning too hotly for anyone to come near it, one abandoned pickup camper. They might also find one dead body, but by now, Shayne thought, everybody else had undoubtedly scattered.

After another moment Canada said quietly, "Seriously?"

"Seriously."

"You arranged it?"

"That particular twist we arranged. The rest more or less just happened."

He left the big highway at the next exit and turned north again at once, remembering a fishermen's turnoff along the canal. After parking, he and Rourke both went in back, leaving the overhead light on so they could all look at each other.

Canada's eyes were rolling, and he was struggling to stay upright.

"If you've got some coffee," he said. "Everything keeps going in and out."

Shayne set the coffeepot back on the stove. Canada

leaned forward, supporting his head in his hands. His nostrils widened as they took in the coffee smell.

"All right, what is it? What's going to happen to me now? The same thing that happened to Eddie Maye? Maybe I'm trying to talk myself into something, but I really doubt it. Mike Shayne? Tim Rourke? It isn't your kind of thing."

"And you may not know Frieda Field," Shayne said. "She's been following Phil Gold around for a couple of weeks."

"She has, has she? I suppose she followed him all the way to Homestead tonight. That's one small point taken care of. You don't know who those people were any more than I do. Let's get back to town."

Shayne laughed. "You still don't understand the situation. If you don't want to think of this as a kidnapping, call it a citizen's arrest. Only we aren't going to turn you over to anybody. This is the whole judicial system right here—state's attorney, grand jury, criminal court. You can claim your constitutional privilege if you want to. That's up to you."

The coffee began to make noises. He filled a cup and gave it to Canada. Frieda looked in the icebox and brought out a coffee cake and a half-dozen hard-boiled eggs.

Canada came fully awake for the first time. He set to work, washing down bites of coffee cake and egg with great slurps of the bitter warmed-up coffee. No one joined him—he so clearly wanted it all. In an amazingly short time, he had consumed the whole cake and all the eggs, and sat back, his eyes bulging.

"Larry, that was interesting to watch," Shayne said.

Canada looked at him evilly. "You don't know a thing about it, do you? Let's hear the rest of the bad news. A citizen's arrest. What are you arresting me for?"

"No particular charge. We think you deserve it, but we haven't been able to come up with anything that will stand up in court. The lawyers won't let Tim print some of his best anecdotes. I didn't plan to kidnap anybody tonight. Somebody else shook that tree, and you fell out. You're right, we probably won't shoot you. We're going to hold you for ransom."

"Come on," Canada said uneasily.

"People have been talking about a million dollars. I think that's a bit high, but you have a wide circle of friends. If they're as loyal as I think they are, I'm sure they can raise it."

"Oh, you're a bastard, Shayne."

"Am I?" Shayne said evenly. "Now I'll tell you what I think about you. You moved into the top slot because the previous guy did something stupid and we put him away for fifteen years. People congratulated me on that, and there was an editorial in Tim's paper. But ask yourself, Larry. Are you any improvement? The same stuff still goes on, with different people. I can be philosophical about that. But I don't want to get you on some petty bribery rap and have somebody else inherit your contracts."

"I never thought of you as a bleeding heart, Shayne."

"No, it's a new thing. As long as you stuck to dope and bookmaking and extortion, you didn't bother me too much. But I don't want you to build that spur through the Everglades."

Canada's eyebrows worked. "If I back out, do you think that will stop it? Hell, no. That's Interstate money, ninety percent federal. It's been approved at the top. If I don't get it, somebody else will."

"This isn't an argument, Larry. We're working out a deal. Who's trying to kill you?"

"Never mind. That kind of thing I take care of myself."

"Maybe I'd better tell you some of the things that happened while you were asleep. I think I'm finally beginning to sort everybody out. I don't have any names yet. I'm hoping you'll help me on that. There seem to be two separate sets of people. They want different things. What's the last thing you remember? The guy with the bullhorn—when he was trying to talk you out in the open, he told you they weren't trying to kill you. That has to be true. Paid hit-men would have cut you down the minute you stepped into the doorway. Now skip a few hours. Everybody thought you were tied to a bed in that trailer. One side wanted to put out the fire. The others wanted to let it burn. And they weren't fooling around. They were shooting at each other."

"I heard shots. I didn't think I was awake. I'm not even sure I'm awake now."

Shayne emptied the coffeepot into his cup. "What would happen if this was a real kidnapping? Does your wife know where you keep your emergency money?"

"No."

"Would she dig it up and hand it over the way loving wives are supposed to?"

Canada moved impatiently. "I don't know what you've heard—"

"That means probably not. How about your number two and your number three men?"

"You've made the point, Goddamn it. They'd go through the motions to make it look good, but there'd be some kind of foul-up. Too bad for Larry."

"Who would get some bullet holes in him and join

Eddie Maye at Woodlawn Park. Yeah, I thought there was more to it than money when you were trying so hard not to be kidnapped back there. And that's why I know you'll be glad to cooperate."

"Put it in English. What happens if I don't?"

"We send the ransom note, giving careful directions about where to deliver the money. We'll be patient. If they can't make the deadline, we'll give them an extension. And when the money's delivered, we'll back away. We'll let them know where they can find you—tied up in the back seat of a car on some back lane. We'll go home and turn on the TV news and see what happens."

Canada wiped his forehead with a napkin. "That's cold-blooded murder."

"It's not exactly cold-blooded, Larry," Shayne said softly. "If we hadn't moved in on that scene in Homestead, it's pretty much the fix you'd be in right now."

Rourke put in, "I don't like to interrupt when you're working, Mike, but I'm not sure I follow. Two separate groups. One wants to grab him so they can raise money on him. And that would be bad for Larry because he can't count on his own people to follow instructions. Or else they come through with the money O.K., but the hit-men get to Larry before anybody else does. Bad either way."

Canada went over his forehead again with the napkin. He seemed to agree with the diagnosis.

Shayne said, "And I think he's ready to fill in a few details. Who's the opposition, Larry? Who's paying those guys who set the trailer on fire?"

"DelSarto?" Rourke suggested when Canada failed to answer. "Bottles Martino?"

"Bottles?" Canada said sharply. "Do you have any reason to—"

"Out of a hat," Rourke said, laughing. "Larry, you're on edge."

"Who wouldn't be? There are guys in town from New York, that much I know. The Eddie May knock-over—what do you think those were, kidnappers? That's what they wanted us to think. Eddie was keeping me posted that there's one certain person who wants all the marbles. And that's hard to defend against, you know? What do you do usually? Put on some extra guards. Travel around with an army until it dies down. But that's the act I'm trying to get away from. I'm trying to say that's all in the past. If I show up at those Tallahassee hearings with my own Secret Service protection, I don't look like your ordinary highway construction man, do I?"

"Let's take a minute on Eddie," Shayne said. "Was he telling you anything you didn't already know?"

"I had my ideas, nothing definite. One name kept popping up. We aren't on the best of terms lately. We've grown apart. He's been seeing my wife on the sly, which is one of the things I happen to know."

"So if we wrap you up and leave you somewhere—"

"And let them know where? I'd weigh fifteen more pounds from the bullets. And you don't call that murder? What do you say, Frieda? You look like a smart girl."

She gave him one of her nicest smiles. "Whatever you call it, the point is, it's believable. It's something any one of us could easily do. Couldn't you in our place?"

"Now the nice guys and the bad guys are all mixed up together. I learn something new about human nature every day. Now we get to the deal. What are you offering me, Shayne?"

"A happy ending in return for some information."

"A lot of information," Rourke corrected him.

Canada tasted the coffee. He wanted it badly, but he wasn't quite able to force it down. "Where do we start?"

"We're still on Eddie Maye. If that wasn't a real kidnapping, what was it?"

"I'd call it a hit, but then I believe in calling things by their right names. He was approached for his support by the people who want to take over. I encouraged him to string them along. He was lining up people for them, supposedly. Collecting funds. Hell, I might as well spell it. DeLuca. Lou DeLuca. I made that guy, brought him up out of nowhere, gave him responsible jobs."

"DeLuca?" Rourke said.

"What's the matter, never heard of him? That's the way Lou likes it. He cooks the books, basically. He counts the money, doesn't do anything about bringing it in. What happened? I'll tell you what happened. That woman Eddie was supposed to be seeing. She was the contact so they wouldn't have to talk direct. Lou found out he was reporting to me, and he had it done. These same New York characters, I wouldn't be too surprised. Not out in the open, that's not how Lou does things. He'd rather sneak anytime. The kidnapping note—window dressing. I don't have the same solid support I did once, but I've still got some debts I can collect around town. He'd know he was in a fight, I can tell you that. So he's tiptoeing. If he can do me the way he did Eddie, fine, all to the good. Is that all you wanted to know? Can I go home now?"

Everybody laughed. He said gloomily, "No, I didn't think so."

"Tim has some questions about the way highways get built in this state," Shayne said. "Who gets paid off how often, how much. Who's been making the real estate money. The Palm Beach interchange would be a good place to start. Tim has it all at the tip of his tongue. Which inspectors look the other way when you go under the specs. We want the whole thing, Larry, from the Tallahassee lobby down to the kickbacks to the Highway Patrol from the tow-truck guys. The insurance deals. The law fees. The sweetheart contracts."

Canada was looking from face to face, very uneasy. "That's asking a hell of a lot."

"I don't think so," Shayne said curtly. "We want you to talk to a tape recorder. Then we'll do a formal version on the typewriter so you can sign it."

"That could get me quite a bundle of years."

"You may decide to go along with the state's attorney and get him to leave your name out of the indictment. Wait and see how it goes. Meanwhile you'll be eating and drinking and enjoying yourself. You can't do any of those things if you're dead."

Frieda said thoughtfully, "I'm beginning to see where you are, Mike. Even if you don't get any convictions, you'll stop the highway."

"You're dreaming," Canada said scornfully. "Once those dotted lines go down on the map, that road is *built*."

"Maybe not this time. You've had the momentum but this could turn it around."

"We've already got the interchanges at both ends for Christ's sake."

"Let them alone for a few years, and the jungle will come back."

"Then that's part of the deal? I don't bid on the new job?"

"No, Larry. We want you to bid, and then we want you to tell us how you rigged it with Gold so you'll turn out to be low."

After a moment Canada said slowly, "I can see I'm not going to be the most popular man in Miami."

"Except with the birdwatchers. They'll give you a certificate. Are you hungry? We can drive to Frieda's and see what she has in the refrigerator. You and Tim can talk on the way."

"I have another coffee cake with only one piece out of it," Frieda said. "Most of a ham."

"Very funny," Canada said bitterly. "I was in a hurry last night, and I only had time for a light supper. I've been rolled around and bounced around and people have been trying to kill me. Now you lay out the terms—the least that can happen, I'm through in the construction business. Goddamn right, I'm hungry."

"We'll drive fast."

"Do that. I want to be home for breakfast. Things to get underway."

"Such as putting people on the street against De-Luca? No, Larry. I want somebody for Eddie Maye. Let's send the ransom note and see what happens."

"I already told you what will happen."

"But wouldn't you like to make sure? Then you'll know who's for and against."

"I was hijacked once. They'll have sense enough not to try it a second time."

"Again, maybe not. They've got a lot invested. If we work it right, we can bring everybody out in the open. Don't worry, Larry. You're our bait, but you're also our one big witness. We don't want to lose you."

Chapter 16

DeLuca didn't get a hell of a lot of sleep. Greco had been told to call him the instant it happened, or the instant it failed to happen. DeLuca kept sitting up in bed to look at the time. He almost wished he had gone along. You couldn't, though. That was the reason for armies, so the general can live to become president of Lockheed or General Dynamics.

His wife asked if he felt like being rubbed. That was her expression for making love. He said no, too much on his mind. He went to sleep finally. A few minutes later the clock went off, bringing him out of a crazy dream in which Canada lay on top of him with his full weight. He almost skipped his exercises this morning. He had never felt less like push-ups and bends. But for five years he had never missed a day, feeling that if he ever started to take it easy he would go all the way, back to cigarettes, back to the days when he was the humble accountant. So he forced himself to complete the full battery.

Greco called from downstairs while he was drinking his vegetable juice. It was O.K.! It had gone according to plan!

DeLuca took the six thousand he still owed the boys and went downstairs. Greco looked as though he had crawled first through a sewer, then through a blackberry thicket. He broke into a happy smile, which DeLuca returned. Mission accomplished, right? DeLuca passed the money and went back to his apartment. He skipped rope hard for fifteen minutes until he was able to stop grinning.

The first thing he did when he got to the office was call a meeting. He was making a list of things to be covered, when a thought struck him. Greco had described the scene in full detail, but before DeLuca went all the way out, he had better make sure.

He called the sheriff's office, identified himself as a UPI man, and asked for confirmation. Indeed, he was told, a thirty-foot trailer had caught fire on the Interstate early that morning. Destruction was total. In the ashes the firemen had discovered the blackened remains of an adult male who had apparently been asleep in one of the bedrooms. A bit taller than average. The pickup that had been hauling the trailer was registered to a man named Allan Vaughan, who happened to be in jail at that moment on drug charges. They were figuring that the rig had been stolen.

When the others arrived, DeLuca, his face grave, announced that their friend Larry Canada had disappeared. His badly smashed Cadillac had been discovered at the Homestead construction site, and all in all, it didn't look good. This might be one of those cases where the body would never be found. DeLuca was sorry to be announcing such bad news because Canada had accomplished a lot and he would be missed. But certain changes, in De Luca's opinion, were overdue. Instead of waiting on further news, he proposed that the changes be put in effect at once.

Whether the others thought he had arranged this himself or was merely taking advantage of Canada's absence, they seemed to accept the way he was taking over. His secretary broke in.

"Molly Canada—she says it's very important. Can you take it?"

"Ask her to hold."

He adjourned the meeting. As soon as the others were out of the office, he took the call.

"He's alive!" Mrs. Canada cried into the phone. "They want one million dollars!"

DeLuca smiled, then erased it quickly so it wouldn't show in his voice. "Now, Molly, somebody's trying to pull something. I'm afraid I've got some bad news. I should have called earlier, but I was hoping against hope—"

"Lou, my God, what are you saying—"

"Get hold of yourself. You knew from the first minute we had to consider the possibility. You know he had enemies."

"*He's dead?*"

"Molly, I'm afraid so. The information I have, the vehicle he was riding in caught on fire, and well, he didn't get out. I couldn't be sorrier. Oh, we had differences, but there was one thing about Larry—nobody could ever accuse him of being anything but totally sincere."

"Lou, his voice sounded so—"

"Sounded, what do you mean, sounded?"

"I got a tape. Lou, a million dollars!"

DeLuca had a good grip on the phone. A tape—when did those construction guys have a minute to make a tape, if they just happened to luck into the kidnapping when they were in there stealing tools? He'd better get over and take charge of that tape so it wouldn't confuse things during the changeover.

"And then on the phone—" she was saying.

"The phone!" DeLuca came out of his chair, and only the force of gravity kept him from going further. "He talked to you on the phone? When?"

"Lou, I'm so—"

"Please, Molly. This is very important."

"Maybe half an hour ago? An hour? He said not to call anybody until I listened to the tape. It was all staticky and there were car noises— It caught fire? Why did it catch fire?"

DeLuca said carefully, "Molly, I'll be there in ten minutes. Make yourself a cup of tea and put some whiskey in it. I'll take care of everything."

He slammed the phone down and left at a run, checking his pace abruptly when he saw that the four men from the meeting were still at the elevator. They rode down together. Two of these men had national connections by kinship and marriage. In theory, they were all Canada's men. If by some crazy chance Canada was still alive, DeLuca's imprudent remarks of a moment ago would be reported back. DeLuca had moved boldly and decisively. As far as these men knew, he couldn't be sure Canada was dead unless he had ordered the killing himself, quite a step for the number man. But to exploit the disappearance without being sure of the death took an equal amount of balls. Either way, DeLuca couldn't back down. He had announced the revolution. It was stomp or be stomped on.

One of them asked if he was keeping up with his tennis.

"Every day." He almost succeeded in smiling. "Maybe I'll have to skip the next couple. Plenty to do!"

They parted on the sidewalk with another round of handshakes and smiles. He drove to the island, and Molly Canada let him in. She had taken his advice about the tea with whiskey in it, omitting the tea. She was shaky on her high heels. She fell toward him and clung. She had a damp Kleenex in her hand, but she might have done that with tap water to make him think she had been crying.

He moved her to the sofa. "Start with the phone call, Molly. You picked up the phone and a voice said, 'This is Larry.' Go on from there."

But she couldn't do it like that. She had to do the full scene, with more Kleenex. He finally extracted the information that the phone conversation had included questions and answers and thus couldn't have been taped in advance. It was definitely her husband's voice, not some clever mimic imitating a dead man. In Greco's version—and what DeLuca was going to do to that kid!—Canada had gone up in flames between two-thirty and three in the morning. Nevertheless, it now seemed, he had been alive at nine, ordering his wife to stay home because a package was going to be delivered and he didn't want her to be off at the beauty parlor. As she said this, Mrs. Canada's hand flew to her hair. What else? That he was the prisoner of some determined and dedicated people who were not to be fooled with.

"And he said one particularly cruel thing," she said with an upward look. "He has all his personal cash in a place nobody can find it, and if anything happens to him, all I'll have is the house, not a single other penny. It was Larry, all right. That was a Larry touch, completely uncalled for."

"Now let's hear the tape," DeLuca said grimly.

The kidnappers had provided not only a cassette, but a tape recorder to play it on. She had trouble with the controls and pressed the erase button by mistake. DeLuca caught it in time.

Canada's voice sounded tired and a little forced, as though he were reading a statement prepared for him by someone else. "I have been kidnapped. I am in serious danger. These are serious people. I have been treated O.K. so far. Do not under any circumstances inform the police. Do not attempt to cut corners or depart from instructions unless you would like to be a widow. Tell Lou DeLuca, nobody else. They want one million dollars. I suggest half from the construction company, half from friends. Fifty- and hundred-dollar bills. Do not try to bait the bills or record serial numbers. Lou has one assignment from me. Get the money together, and don't try any fancy stuff, there is no way it can be done. At four-thirty exactly, four-thirty on the dot, Lou will come out of our house with the money in a suitcase. *Alone.* Drive slowly to the south parking lot of Miami High School. There he will find a red pickup. It will be equipped with a citizen-band radio. Do not change channels, Lou. Turn it on. Drive west on 395 at exactly forty miles per hour. You will receive further instructions by radio. If anybody does anything foolish, like being a half hour late or a couple of thousand short, three things will happen. I will be shot. You will be shot, Molly. And Lou will be shot.

That's what they promise, and I believe them. If there aren't any snags, I'll be home for supper. Make something good."

"I think chicken crêpes," she said. "He loves them. Chocolate cake."

The chimes sounded while DeLuca was rewinding the tape. This was a special-delivery letter, which Molly signed for and tore open breathlessly. It contained stale news. Her man had been kidnapped and the price was a million. The one interesting thing was that the note was almost a copy of the Eddie Maye one—same ink, same style. It was out of sequence, it should have arrived before the phone call. But that was the post office for you.

DeLuca had to rush if he wanted to meet the deadline. And having heard that his name was number three on the kill list, he was no longer thinking about sabotaging the collection. Canada himself had probably contributed that suggestion—quick thinking, Larry. DeLuca would have to hand over the full sum. If he had anything to say about what happened after that, however, Canada wouldn't be alive to eat supper.

He gave Molly a quick, sympathetic hug and told her he would keep in touch. Flushed and excited, a little drunk, she was much more attractive today than he had ever seen her. He took both the tape and the recorder because he was going to be pitching to some very suspicious people. Cash was the problem. There would be notes to arrange, signatures to get. DeLuca himself, to maintain his new status, would have to contribute a tenth.

His first stop was the Doral. After the busy night, Greco had decided to stay over. A girl in unbuttoned pajamas came to the door to see who was being so insistent. Greco was all but asleep, smiling blissfully while another girl chewed at him. Nick didn't seem to be home, though that bed had been slept in. DeLuca picked a gun off the carpet and used it to drive the girls into the hall, throwing their clothes after them. Greco was up on his elbows.

"Hey, man—"

DeLuca swung, and he dodged back. "I don't see why—" he whined.

"What gave you the funny idea Canada was in that trailer? Did you see him?"

"Not with my own eyes, no, but those other guys, one of them, looked in and saw him. If he said it once, he said it a couple of times. I wouldn't shit you! Would I still be here? I'd be in Mexico."

"Where's your tall friend?"

"Well, Nick—he got shot and I had to put him in the fire."

DeLuca nodded. "Not as heavy as Canada, but about the same height."

Greco, paling, went even deeper into the pillow. He looked at the gun in DeLuca's hand and began to babble. "I didn't, honest—"

He ended up in a fetal coil. DeLuca, disgusted, ordered him into a cold shower. In a pillow case, where Greco had hidden them from the girls, he found the six big ones he had paid for the job. Becoming impatient almost at once, he rolled up his sleeve, went in, and dragged Greco out of the shower. The big question was, who were the three people who had driven off with the trailer? All Greco knew was that they had definitely been after Canada. The name of Canada had been mentioned over and over. He would swear to that.

To bring his anger under control, DeLuca forced

himself to unwrap a stick of gum slowly and deliberately and chew it down.

"Well, you blew it," he told the boy, shivering in the chill blast of the air-conditioning. "This has been embarrassing for me, and if that slob comes home, it could be a lot more than embarrassing. I feel like blasting you, I really do, and start over with somebody else."

"Please—"

In fact, DeLuca was strongly tempted. The trouble was, the recruiting and briefing would all take time, and he shouldn't even be here, he should be out accumulating the ransom.

"I'm going to give you one more crack. Better not fuck up twice. Stay here. No women. Be awake and dressed and straight by three-thirty."

Chapter 17

Shayne, back in his own car, met the bondsman in Homestead. Half an hour later the man brought out the construction workers, Benjamin and Vaughan, who had been arrested the night before for the possession of heroin.

Shayne unlatched his rear door and said he would drive them to work. "I'm Michael Shayne. I'm a friend of Soupy Simpson. Which one of you is Benjamin?"

The stockier man nodded slightly. They were both in their thirties, in need of a shave and a shower, wearing work pants and dirty T-shirts. Shayne had two cartons of take-out coffee and a box of doughnuts. That convinced them he was friendly. They got in the car.

"That stuff was planted on us," Benjamin said.

"Three ounces, they tell me. That's a lot to invest in

a practical joke." He passed them the coffee. "I'd lik
to watch your reactions, but I've got to be moving. E
erybody seems to think you've been stealing constru
tion equipment on a regular basis. True or false?"

Benjamin took a swallow of coffee. "We'll plead
that when the time comes."

"That won't be the charge. The rap is much worse
The traffic light changed, and he moved. "First-degre
murder."

One of the men said softly, "How do you make th
out?"

"Somebody hit the Homestead job last night an
took everything that wasn't nailed down. It all ende
up in your trailer."

"Why don't you talk to Soupy about that? Tal
money."

"As soon as Soupy understands what he's mixed u
in," Shayne said, "I think he'll be hard to get hold o
I'd give you the same advice, except that you're in a l
deeper. But I think I see a way you can dig yourse
out. That's why I put up your bail."

"Out of the kindness of your heart," one of the me
said ironically. "Now you want a return favor. Firs
degree murder. Who was murdered?"

"Two people. Eddie Maye, a loan shark, a kidnap
ping attempt that misfired. Somebody else burned
death in your trailer. He hasn't been identified yet.
think they'll find he was also shot in the stomacl
which helped. One other thing. The big boss was ki
napped."

"*Canada?*"

"That's right, a big fish, and they want a big pric
for him. Apparently the kidnapping and robbery too
place at pretty much the same time. The police hav
decided both crimes were committed by the same pe

ple. Canada was meeting somebody in the command trailer. A secret meeting, highly confidential, and the other person won't step forward to admit it happened unless he absolutely has to. You were working with Canada in a pilfering racket. People will say you set up that meeting to report or pass money, got him out there, and grabbed him. Now for the next step, the big one. There isn't much doubt the Canada kidnappers are also the Eddie Maye kidnappers. It's one of those things where you're going to be presumed guilty unless you can prove yourself innocent. How does it sound, pretty rough?"

"We've been in the tank most of the night. We haven't been running around mailing ransom notes."

"Nobody thinks you did it all single-handed. You'd have somebody outside to handle the messages. Maybe you even set up the bust yourself so you'd have a fixed address overnight."

Both men protested the absurdity of the idea, and Shayne went on, "When they rake through the ashes, they're going to find a payloader wheel, an acetylene tank, a welding torch, and a lot else. They'll trace it back. I happen to know where you got it. You got it from Soupy, and Soupy got it from me. You don't have to understand how that happened, just how it looks, and it looks bad. So I know you've already made up your mind to help."

For a moment there was nothing from the back seat, not even the sound of swallowing.

"How?" Benjamin said then.

After dropping the construction workers, Shayne called the bowling alley and asked for Soupy Simpson.

"Another moneymaking opportunity," Shayne told him. "I'm paying three hundred for this, and you may be able to milk it at the opposite end. I want to plant a story so every cop in town above the rank of patrolman will hear about it before noon. I want to start it in three places—Miami, Miami Beach, and the sheriff's office. How are your connections?"

"Good in all three. Go ahead, Mike, I'm listening."

"Larry Canada has been snatched. His wife had a phone call so we know he's alive. The asking price is one million, and Lou DeLuca is raising it. The deadline is four-thirty. They're under strong pressure to keep the cops out of it."

"And you want the cops in on it?"

"One certain cop. I don't know which one."

"Larry Canada snatched, one million, DeLuca."

"Don't leave out the phone call—Canada himself talking."

"Got it. Mike, can you hand-deliver the money? I was listening to the morning news. A dead man in a trailer. I think I'll take a little vacation."

"Good idea. I was about to suggest it."

Jack Downey was in bad shape. He dropped a couple of speed-up pills, and usually that was enough to enable him to get through the day. Today it merely had the effect of making everything spin. It was an ordinary Miami day, sunshine through smog, but the light hurt his eyes. It seemed to Downey that everybody looked at him strangely. He shouldn't have been so greedy. Why hadn't he settled for the small gain? He was a small man, what was wrong with small money? The details of the night were already beginning to recede. Those kooks, Werner and Pam, had talked him into it, and then when the going got rough, they ran.

After some bad experiences with partners, who invariably let him down, he had made his superiors acknowledge that he worked better alone. All they were interested in was results, and Downey got those, although it was fair to say that lately he had lost some of his edge. He had some paper work to get out of the way before he could coop up for the day. He was fighting the typewriter, making mistake after mistake, when Soupy Simpson called.

Downey stood up so abruptly that he sent the typewriter table squealing back against the next desk. The man there looked at him curiously. Downey asked Soupy a few low questions. It was a rumor, that was all, but Soupy had heard it from several sources, and he thought Downey might be interested, not that he saw any connection with the other thing Downey had been asking about the night before, the pilferage thing.

"A phone call?" Downey said. "To the wife?"

"That's what Lou DeLuca is saying. He has a tape he's playing for people."

Downey thanked Soupy for thinking of him, then sat down and tried to finish the form. After four wrong strikes in a row, he yanked the damn thing out of the machine and filed it. Alive? Of course Canada wasn't alive. This was some kind of con. He put on his harness and left without telling anyone where he was going. He didn't know himself. It sometimes helped just to get in the car and go.

Using an outside booth, he called a friend in the sheriff's office and asked if they had anything new on the burned-out trailer. No identification yet; they were trying to get a dental chart, but the teeth were scattered all over. Downey drove a few blocks, pulled up at another phone, and called the Homestead barracks. Benjamin and Vaughan, in spite of having been caught with three bags of pure, were out on $10,000 bail. What did it mean?

Canada lived on one of the man-made bay islands, with good security at the bottleneck leaving the causeway. The bottleneck couldn't exclude cops, however, and Downey arrived in time to see Lou DeLuca come out of the house carrying a tape recorder. Downey considered giving him a fast frisk and a little pushing around, but decided he was too far down to know anything. He was the messenger boy, that was all. Downey rang the doorbell. The door was chained, and Mrs. Canada wouldn't let him in.

He set off again and presently noticed that his car had taken him to the Interstate. Maybe the car knew something he didn't. He went south to Homestead and in through the site. If you knew where to look, you could see signs of what had happened. A couple of official-looking cars were parked at the command trailer. Otherwise they were making highway as usual, noisily, under the usual cloud of dust.

Downey drove out the opposite end, made a forbidden U, and headed toward Miami Heights. He had a bet going. If his colleagues weren't there, he would call it all off, the hell with it, it was too risky to attempt alone. But they were there. Werner was packing, and Pam was on the bed, wearing nothing to speak of and smoking a joint. Downey picked it out of her hand and drew on it deeply.

"We said goodbye," she said.

"This may not be over yet."

"Will you get out of here?" Werner said, with that funny mildness he had been putting on for the last couple of days.

With no change of expression, perfectly calm, Downey hit him twice, once in the kidneys, again at the hinge of the jaw. He put every ounce of his frustration into the punches. Ten years earlier he would have done some hospital damage. Werner went back on the bed, arms and legs splayed, looking surprised, but he stayed conscious.

"They had a phone call," Downey said, "from Canada himself. So the son of a bitch wasn't in that trailer after all. Now shut up and listen. Don't ask me who was doing that shooting last night. All I know is, I got one of them good, in the gut. What I'm wondering, are those his bones in that trailer? I swear I saw Canada in there, at least I saw something. But hell, the visibility—maybe they set it up to *look* fat like Canada, and maybe he was somewhere else all the time."

"You saw him breathing," Pam said.

"Let's not rake it all up. We all make mistakes."

He was feeling dizzy, and he had to sit down. He had worked it out in the car, but under Pam's skeptical look it began slipping away.

"I just came from the site. A couple of places where he might be, like a stretch of conduit, and there's that whole swamp country around there. I'm not saying we ought to go out and look. We wouldn't know where to begin. We don't care about Canada—write that off. The money's the thing. Listen, remember that payloader?"

"I'll never forget."

"I found out this morning that Benjamin, one of the guys who ripped off the stuff, is a *payloader driver*. That's pretty conclusive."

"They're in jail."

"Not anymore they're not. Somebody bailed them. They stashed Canada somewhere, in a junked car or wherever, and he's still there, isn't he? They wouldn't have time yet to move him. Now if I was in their shoes,

I'd go to work as though nothing happened. They're working overtime on that highway job, to seven or eight most days. Four-thirty is when they want the money to be ready. They'll slip off to go to the john or something, pick up the dough, however they've got it arranged, hide it, and get back on the job. That's guesswork, but it fits the facts. So what we do, we work on it on both ends. The money guy's somebody nobody ever heard of, DeLuca. He's my responsibility. You guys get over to the site and watch the exits, keep an eye out for Vaughan and Benjamin. We'll rig up something good. When they go looking for the money, it may not be there. Or we'll let them pick it up, put on the masks, and take it away, whichever. I'm not talking nickels now. I'm talking a million bucks."

They didn't see any of this as clearly as he did. The more he argued, the realer it looked. It took him over an hour to get them out of the house. At the end he was talking wildly, hardly knowing what he was saying.

He drove back to the site, showed his badge to the foreman, and asked him to identify a whole string of names, made up on the spot except for Benjamin and Vaughan. Vaughan was a dump-truck driver, in and out. Benjamin, the payloader guy, was working back and forth between the gravel pile and the hot plant.

Downey deployed his troops. He wanted them both to be really invisible, which meant they had to have a legitimate reason for being here. Downey attached his own police blinker to the roof of their rented Ford. With that long hair, Werner was hard to believe as a cop, so Downey bullied him to a Homestead barber, who cut a lot of it off. It changed his appearance completely. He looked like a detective Downey knew—that man, too, looked angry most of the time.

He drove Pam to the top of the site, where dump

trucks bringing in sand and gravel had to cross the highway. A flag girl in a yellow hat and bright orange vest brought the traffic to a halt to let them pass.

Downey stopped beside her. "We got a call from your family, dear. Do you have your own car?"

"What do you mean? Is anything wrong?"

"Some kind of accident. She was so hysterical I couldn't make out. Your dad? Somebody."

The girl's hand went to her mouth. "Is it bad?"

"She was leaving for the hospital. She wants you to go straight home."

The girl was already untying her vest. "Oh, God. That's a two-hour drive. Did she say what hospital?"

"Just to go home. Somebody'll be there by then."

"Now isn't that just like my mom?" the girl cried. "I'll be worrying all the day. Dad—he drives like a crazy person. I hope it's not too bad."

Pam put on the vest and hat and accepted the flag. Downey drove off with the girl.

Chapter 18

After counting the money, and counting it again to be sure he'd been right the other times, DeLuca had a final exchange with Canada's wife.

"Lou, you'll be careful?" She put a moist hand on his arm. "You won't provoke them? Because he meant that. You know Larry, he wouldn't put his money in any obvious place. I'll bet you it's in the Bahamas someplace. If anything goes wrong I'll never find it."

"If anything goes wrong," DeLuca said, "it won't be Lou DeLuca's fault. I want to stay alive myself, you know. Most of this dough is other people's. If Larry lives through, he'll pay them back. Otherwise they're out. So I'm going to play this strictly according to the book."

Her hold tightened. "Lou, you've been such a good

friend today. When this is over, I hope we can see each other more. You don't know how lonely it's been."

He stood on the front doorstep for a moment to let anybody who was watching see that, as instructed, he was completely alone. Then he drove to the Miami High School, on Twenty-fourth Avenue. He had played the tape for a number of people during the day, but he had always cut if off at the point where it started to get specific. He didn't want anybody lying in wait along the way. He was the only one who knew he was going to change cars. He spotted the pickup at once. A Chevy several years old, it had been used hard. Empty beer bottles were rolling under the seat. He turned on the radio. It was set on Channel 19, but was producing nothing but frying noises.

As he went up the westbound ramp of the East–West Expressway, he saw his man Greco swing into place behind him. Greco was driving a Honda 750, a machine he claimed to know intimately, and DeLuca hoped this wasn't more of his New York bullshit. He was concealed behind dark glasses and a wraparound crash helmet. Only his nose showed. He was wearing a black leather jacket studded with rivets and emblems. DeLuca knew he would be followed and watched. Any kind of automobile escort would be spotted at once. But except to motorcycle lovers, all motorcycles look more or less alike. Under the black jacket, Greco wore another that was white and silver, the on-the-road uniform of a club that called itself Ghouls on Wheels. At some stopping point he could discard the top jacket and become a new person. Later, if necessary, he could throw that jacket away and ride in a striped tank shirt—still another identity.

At forty everybody was passing DeLuca. Greco

zoomed by without a look, then throttled back and stayed within sight.

The frying noise stopped. A voice said abruptly, "DeLuca. If you can hear me, blink your lights."

The dashboard radio had no transmitter. Apparently they didn't want to be bothered with stupid questions. He snapped the lights on and off. The voice told him to hold his speed and turn south at the interchange.

He signaled in plenty of time. Greco went down first, pulling off at the bottom to look at a road map. By the time he showed up in DeLuca's mirror again, DeLuca was beginning to miss him. He was no longer an Angel, and was now a Ghoul on Wheels. He kept a good interval.

Twenty minutes went by. They were approaching Homestead. The voice said suddenly, "DeLuca. Pull off the highway. Set your blinkers."

Startled, DeLuca signaled and pulled over. The traffic streamed by—two Detroit sedans, a big Dodge Sportsman with a bike mounted behind, the white and silver Ghoul on his Honda.

"There's a cooler in back," the radio said. "Bring it up in the cab. Do that right now."

The cooler was a battered Styrofoam box with a centered handle and a clamp at each end. There were two stickers on it, one a playful leaping dolphin, the identifying emblem of the Miami football team. The other sticker had been there a long time and had partially eroded: "—allace for President."

"DeLuca. You know what we want you to do now. Transfer the money. Then get going."

DeLuca unclamped the lid. Several loose cans stood in a shallow drawerlike compartment. He lifted that out and stacked the money in the body of the cooler.

He hesitated for a fraction of a second, holding the last two packages of hundreds. Would they call everything off if the count was a little short? Probably not, but what the hell. He tossed them in.

He clamped the lid on and returned to the highway, shifting up fast because he didn't want Greco to get too far ahead of him.

The voice said, "DeLuca. Pull off at the rest area. You'll see a beat-up Pontiac with the door open. Don't be in a rush. Plenty of time. When there's nobody around, put the cooler in. Drive to the next exit, come back the opposite way, stop at the rest area on that side. Next exit, come back, first rest area. We'll contact you if we get the right total. Turn on your lights if you understand. Flick them on and off if you want the instructions repeated."

DeLuca put on his lights and left them on. Now if the kid had had the sense to pull over and wait—

It was early for supper stops, and there were only three or four trucks at the rest area, one or two cars, the van that had passed DeLuca on the road, Greco's motorcycle. Greco had his tool kit open and was pretending to make some minor repair. The parking strip was a long arc going in among trees, with barbecue grills and picnic tables, a few strange-looking pieces of sculpture. The comfort station, at the high point of the arc, was a glazed brick structure with a map of southern Florida's points of interest on the wall of the entryway.

DeLuca took the cooler to the nearest picnic table and opened a beer. As soon as he was sure that only Greco was watching, he put the cooler in the Pontiac and jumped into the pickup. He scrawled a quick note: "Kill five minutes. First rest area, northbound." He took off.

Greco appeared in the mirror before he reached the exit. Now that the money had been delivered, DeLuca didn't think he would be watched so closely, but he went on being careful. At the bottom of the exit ramp, he let the note flutter out of the window and made the turns that started him back to Miami.

Both rest areas were in the same general vicinity, but not directly across the highway from each other. DeLuca parked. Now he would find out how efficient these people were. In the same suitcase in which he had carried the money, he had a long-barreled German Luger, equipped with a silencer, a killer's weapon. He checked the load and put the pistol on the seat beside him.

Greco pulled in. It was the same helmet, the same machine, but a different motorcyclist, in a striped sleeveless shirt. He put the bike on his kick stand and went inside to relieve himself.

The radio continued to sputter without saying anything intelligible. The wait stretched to ten minutes, fifteen.

Then the voice said, "DeLuca. On the button, give or take a few hundred. That's lucky because we've been right on your taillights all the way. Now you'll want to know where to find the fat man. Don't worry, he's fine. A little hungry, is all. He'll give you a big wet kiss, and Miami can get back to normal. He's seven miles south. Stay on the Interstate till you hit the construction. One-point-three miles after you go one-way, you'll see a flag girl and truck access in on your left. There's a lot of confusion, but here's what you do. Go to the big mixing tank and face east. There are two portable toilets. You'll see one right away to your left by the equipment trailer. That's not the one. The other's over behind the gravel. It's padlocked. A sign says,

'Out of Order, Do Not Use.' Your man is inside, and that seat isn't upholstered, DeLuca, so he'll be happy to hear your voice. One last word, Lou. Thanks loads."

A portable toilet. Perfect. DeLuca's pulse was banging in triple time. He already had his motor started, as though he were in a hurry, but of course he wasn't in that much of a hurry because he wanted Greco to show up first. Greco kicked his machine to life and spun away. DeLuca stayed behind him. Approaching the exit, he used his blinker, and Greco made the turn first. Nobody followed them off. They stopped side by side in the underpass, directly under the big highway. DeLuca, watching the mirrors, repeated the instructions he had been given.

"A good place for a clean hit. First make damn sure he's in there. Then shoot through the wall. It's noisy as hell, nobody'll know *nothing*. Let's do it right, use the whole clip."

He passed Greco the gun and two extra clips. "I want witnesses when I find him. I'll stop for a couple of cops. You'll have five minutes. Find the toilet, make sure he's inside, shoot, then go."

"Won't it be kind of out in the open?"

"Back of the gravel pile, they said. They wouldn't leave him there in front of everybody. Sort of lean down and camouflage it. And if you're as good on that sickle as you say you are, nobody's going to catch you."

Werner had pulled off near the southern exit, his Ford wearing the borrowed police flasher. It was a good place for a cop car, and nobody gave him a look. Traffic here funneled down to one lane and a crossover. For the next hour, while Werner sagged over the wheel in a half doze, knowing that Downey was totally out of his mind and nothing would happen, the trucks kept to their pattern and no private cars left the lot. Then a rusted-out Pontiac went by. Werner covered the lower half of his face. The man at the wheel was Benjamin!

Benjamin's payloader continued to gnaw at the gravel. He was sneaking out the back way so his absence wouldn't be noticed. Downey had been right after all! It had been amateur night all around. They themselves were amateurs, and Benjamin and Vaughan were amateurs. They had stumbled all over each other.

Werner began shaking suddenly. He got that under control by doing something no genuine cop ever does in public—bending over and touching his toes. He broke the suction holding the blinker to his roof, threw it in back, and slipped unobtrusively into the line of traffic.

The Pontiac was taking no special precautions. It pulled into a rest area, and Werner followed it in. Benjamin was built like his own payloader—solid and chunky. In a hurry to get to the men's room, he left one of the Pontiac's doors open behind him. Werner, anticipating a long afternoon, had brought sandwiches and Coke. He took them to a picnic table.

Presently a red pickup pulled in and parked near the Pontiac. Werner disposed of his trash and went to look at the map at the entrance to the washrooms. It told him what roads to take to the Monkey Jungle, Coral Reef State Park, the Serpentarium, the Miami Wax Museum, and Vizcaya. Meanwhile a dark, carefully dressed man, whose clothes didn't go with the banged-up pickup, carried a cooler to a table and removed a beer. He drank it slowly. Then, instead of putting the

cooler back in the pickup, he put it in the Pontiac—the
money!—walked to the end of the paved strip, returned to the pickup, and drove off.

Werner gave everybody a couple of minutes. Before
following, he put the blinker back on.

What would Benjamin do now? Count the money
and return to work, obviously, take over the payloader,
and finish out the day. He wouldn't pass it to anybody.
If they had another confederate, he would have been
used to make the collection. So they had time to work
something out, and this time their plan could be fool-
proof.

Downey, in a police helicopter, followed the pickup
all the way, crossing and recrossing in a loose weave.
Approaching Homestead, there was considerable
traffic from the air base, and it was possible to hang
right behind. As soon as he saw the pattern take shape,
he tapped the pilot's shoulder and pointed to the
ground. The pilot put him down in a field. He walked
to his car.

Shayne kept the payloader in action while Benjamin
was gone. The Pontiac returned and parked at the high
end of the lot near the locked toilet. Approaching the
payloader, Benjamin took an exuberant little stutter
step to show Shayne it had gone well.

"Who saw you?" Shayne said when Benjamin
climbed to the cab.

"They all looked normal to me. Kid on a motorbike,
couple of truck drivers."

Frieda was in the cab of a second payloader. Using
a channel far down the band, Shayne told her the
cooler was back. Benjamin had made a rough count,
and it all seemed to be there. Tim Rourke, in Frieda's

van on the highway, had his citizen's band set to the same channel, and Shayne told him to signal DeLuca that the count was acceptable and he could proceed to the toilet and free the prisoner. Still a fourth radio was part of this hook-up. It was inside the toilet, heavily muffled with rags.

Frieda's payloader moved. A haphazardly parked car, Shayne's own, left only one exit from the parking lot, past the toilet, into the main cross-site road below Shayne's payloader. A short lateral movement would close the trap. Six county cops waited in the command trailer.

Shayne started the countdown. DeLuca was seven minutes away.

"There's a bike," Benjamin said, craning. "A Honda! It's the same—no, that guy was wearing a club jacket."

The motorcyclist, a short figure in a striped undershirt, came all the way through, then turned toward the parked cars.

"Frieda?" Shayne called.

"I see him. A motorcycle could be a problem."

Shayne called the cops in the trailer and directed them to move two cars to the highway.

"Don't shoot him. We want to ask him some questions."

The motorcycle, kicking gravel, went in among the cars, out the far side, and came back, to stop near the Pontiac after a short, tight skid. Usually a motorcyclist's first move after dismounting is to take off his helmet. This one kept his on. Straddling his machine, he looked the site over deliberately, slapping his leg with a pair of driving gauntlets. He could only be seen from the payloaders, which continued to charge forward and draw back, forward and back. The hot plant was grinding slowly with a hideous clanking. Hot trucks moved out, carrying loads of freshly cooked asphalt to the paver, which was inching almost imperceptibly south. A heavy crane was swinging one of the big cross culverts into place. More trucks came and went continually with gravel and sand. Pickups darted about, seemingly at random. The afternoon sun slanted in through the haze.

The motorcyclist moved to the toilet, as though to read the sign on the door. Shayne put his lips to the transmitter and groaned. Benjamin looked around in surprise. Shayne groaned again, then made muffled breathing sounds through his hand.

Chapter 19

Greco had played playground basketball as a kid, before he stopped growing, and he could remember days
when he knew he couldn't be stopped. Everything he
threw toward the basket had to go in. When you felt
that way, he discovered, it had generally happened.
You could make impossible shots.

He hadn't liked the idea when he first heard it from
DeLuca, but now, after looking it over, it almost
seemed to be arranged with the hit-man in mind. The
toilet was surprisingly private. Noisy, DeLuca had said.
The place was so noisy he could have got away without
using the silencer. One quick look had shown him six
possible exits. Bang, bang, bang. And when DeLuca
showed up with the cops, they would find that the kidnappers had tricked them. Not wanting to take any

chances, the bastards had drilled Canada after making him dictate the tape.

All the same, Greco intended to take full credit for this. By then DeLuca would be established. He wouldn't be hurt by rumors.

Greco was carrying the gun in one of the gauntlets, the long barrel poking into the middle finger. He eased it out to be sure the silencer hadn't caught. Then he noticed the Pontiac. Greco had a good eye for the different makes and models, and he knew at once that this was the car that had picked up the money. He sauntered in that direction. Sure enough, there was the white Styrofoam box on the front seat, sitting there right out in the open, looking so tempting, with the familiar friendly dolphin on the lid. The car would be locked, probably? Yes, the windows were closed, the lock buttons were down.

The dust got to him all at once. He was having difficulty breathing. What did they expect him to do, leave it for somebody else? That wouldn't be human nature. He owed it to Nick, who had done so well in the night. It would give his death some meaning. DeLuca would be so delighted to see it again, he might be willing to split it down the middle, half to DeLuca, half to Greco.

He decided to do it. He'd feel like such a schmuck if he didn't. Of course, he had to shoot up the toilet first. When he started something, he finished.

After looking around again, he moved to the tall portable box. He distinctly heard movement inside, breathing, a muffled moan. After reading the notice on the door, he put on a little act for anybody who might be watching, as though he had to take a leak and couldn't hold it any longer. He went behind the toilet and took out his whang, which was a little shriveled from all the excitement.

He waited for the flow to commence before firing. Through the thin metal, he heard impact, a grunt: a hit on the first shot. DeLuca had wanted all eight. Greco gave him all eight, stitching a random pattern inside the strike zone, a rectangle between two feet and five feet from the floor. High and inside, high and outside, a slider low and away. That man was now *dead*.

He finished his piss, snapped in a new clip, and put everything away, the gun and his cock. The payloaders were still going, the trucks going and coming. Returning to the Pontiac, he smashed a window, unlocked the door, and lifted out the cooler. It was pleasantly heavy. He strapped it on his rear rack.

The basketball feeling was now extremely intense. He kicked off. Instead of using one of the traveled paths, he went over a bank, swerved at the bottom, recovered, and headed for the south road.

The motorcycle gave him a dreamlike feeling of power. It was a real brute. He could fly from the fastest cars. But first he had to get out in the open, and one of the payloaders was rolling at him. Seeing no way to get through, he spun all the way around, hitting the ground with one foot. They didn't like outsiders, was the only explanation. They couldn't be after him yet. He saw an opening and went under one of the belts at the hot plant, between the belt and the gears. He gave a high, crazy laugh and a wave. Who was he? One of those nutty bikers from Miami out to bug the straight people, run a few obstacles, and be on his way. He got a wry shake of the head from one of the truck drivers, who had to respect machismo even in this freakish form.

Now he had a straight run to the highway, but to continue the show, he dodged between trucks and then, taking what he realized immediately afterward was one hell of a chance, rode through a loose section of culvert lying around waiting to be laid.

He saw DeLuca's pickup coming in. He wouldn't stop to talk, but he wanted to convey a message: Canada was dead, Greco had recovered the money. He detoured so DeLuca would be sure to see the box on the back of the bike. Light flashed from the pickup's windshield. He couldn't see DeLuca's face, but the look of the truck itself told him he was being naïve. Pickups are plain and practical. For DeLuca the practical thing to do would be to take the cooler and tell Greco to go screw himself, here's five hundred, buy yourself a drink. Down the middle? Don't be silly. And for the first time Greco realized that the Styrofoam box an inch from his ass was filled with real money, which anybody could spend. You could be any age, at any level. Your name could be Greco.

He headed straight between the truck's headlights. He saw the truck's brakes take hold, and he spun out and around. DeLuca shouted a question. Greco pushed the leather glove into the open window. DeLuca reached, thinking Greco was giving him something. And Greco was. He was giving him death. He fired through the finger. The upward shot shattered the lower half of DeLuca's face.

Greco was past, a rich man. He gave another wild hoot and wound into the next higher gear.

Nothing was ahead but a truck road and the flag girl. For no rational reason, merely to show her authority, she was waving her flag at him. She thought she could stop him with that puny flag? He decided to make her jump. Nice-looking cunt. Greco liked long hair on a girl, those skinny flanks.

She pointed her flag, and he was struck a powerful blow on the chest, which knocked him backward out of his seat. One foot caught, and he stayed with the motorcycle. The heavy machine, no longer a friend, whipped around and came over on top of him. His scream rang back and forth inside the helmet like the screaming of more than one person. They slid twenty feet together, Greco and the Honda, through rising dust. When they came to rest, he was looking straight at the sun, but he was unable to close his eyes.

When Werner saw the motorcycle stop near the Pontiac, he started his motor and turned on the rooftop flasher. Of course, the kidnappers could have told somebody to come and pick up the cooler, but why would they do that when it could leave unobtrusively with Benjamin himself at the end of the day?

One of the payloaders was moving erratically. Suddenly the motorcycle burst out of the dust, with the cooler strapped to the rack. It disappeared and appeared again, playing games near the hot plant. Werner was moving. The motorcycle broke free, nearly colliding with a pickup—*the* pickup, he realized—then seemed to hit an obstruction at a bad angle and flipped. Werner drove up. Pam whirled.

"He's got the money!"

Werner jumped out and quickly broke open the buckles. The dust from the spill was still in the air around him. Straightening, he took one step toward his car. Cars were moving out from the hot plant. A sand truck was coming in to cross. Werner had come in a police car and so was obviously a cop. But a real cop wouldn't take off again an instant after arriving at the scene of an accident this bad. He couldn't make up his mind. And he was still standing there, holding the cooler, being pulled in several directions at once, when the sand truck came up. The driver looked at the fallen motorcycle. The front wheel was folded. The biker, covered with blood, looked almost as battered as his machine and considerably more fragile.

"Jesus Christ," the truck driver said. "I've got a kid myself who wants one of those Hondas. Not with my money! Anything I can do?"

"We'll take care of it," Werner told him.

The truck pulled past, and Werner swung the cooler over the tailgate into the sand. It slid down the cone-shaped pile, out of sight from below.

Pam was trembling badly. Werner's move with the cooler—whether that was smart or dumb, there was no way to call it back now—had caused him to unfreeze. He looked into the pickup. What he saw there drove him back several steps. Before he could freeze again, he snatched Pam's gun and threw it into the front seat beside the dead man.

"Don't tell Downey," he said. "Half million for you. Half million for me. Fuck him. You don't know a thing!"

Pam began shuddering, taking deep breaths and letting them out on a rising note. That was all right. She had witnessed a double shooting, and nobody would be surprised if she came slightly unglued. And all at once her orange vest seemed to break open from inside. Blood spurted out. The motorcyclist on the ground was holding his long gun in both hands. The barrel wavered and fell back.

Werner was too late to catch Pam as she fell. The yellow hat went bouncing away. He turned her over. After the first hard spurt, the blood was welling out of her chest like a pool overflowing. She tried to speak. Bubbles came out. He let her down. He wasn't thinking of her at all, he was thinking about the money.

He clapped on her hard hat and automatically

stopped being a cop and changed into a construction worker. He ran toward the cars, gesturing.

"They shot—killed—"

There were enough other things to look at so he got away with it. Other cars gathered. He doubled over and was sick in the dirt. It was real bile, real vomit. Very pale, his hand to his mouth, he turned his back to the confused scene and walked away. His rented car with the flasher would be left over when everything got sorted out. That would be hours from now. No one would make the connection.

He walked all the way through. Without looking to see who was watching, he crossed the access road and the highway. He made a wide detour through the tangled undergrowth, going into swamp water up to his knees, and circled back. A great irrigation conduit ran under the road at this point. He ducked down and went in, walking through a tiny sluggish trickle of water. The second half of the conduit had been tied in, but not yet covered with dirt.

He stopped several feet short of the mouth, in dark shadow. He could see the sand pile. The dump trucks were feeding the pile on the opposite side from the payloader.

Shayne, in the payloader cab, was a half mile from the action, his view partly obscured by the moving dust. He gave quiet instructions to the sheriff's deputies. One police car, its blinker working, was on its way in from the highway. He was outside the cab, about to drop to the ground, when Benjamin called him back. He was in time to see the Honda and a pickup apparently collide. The Honda flipped and threw its rider. A sand truck crossed the highway, paused, and went on. Shayne's was the fourth car to reach the scene. De-

Luca and the man he had imported to kill Canada had shot and killed each other, and the flag girl had been hit during the exchange. She was dying. The Styrofoam cooler was no longer strapped to the motorcycle.

These deaths were sheriff's business, and the deputies had already begun the lengthy process of picking up. Shayne took the ranking deputy aside and asked for permission to search the pickup and the cars.

The man gave him a hard look. "This is your show, Mike. Go ahead, but you know we're going to need a lot more than you've given us so far. Am I permitted to ask what you're looking for?"

"The Styrofoam cooler that was on the back of the Honda."

"A beer cooler? Three people are dead here, Mike. They weren't arguing about beer."

"Probably not," Shayne agreed.

Two feet by one foot by a foot and a half, the cooler would be a hard thing to conceal. By the time Frieda arrived, Shayne had decided it must have bounced off the carrier during the jolting ride. But Frieda was sure it had still been on the motorcycle when it sheared away from the pickup and went down.

"We were facing the wrong way, with the bucket up. I lost track of him when he went under the belts. When he came out in the open again, the first thing I looked for was the cooler. It was definitely there, Mike."

Shayne looked at the tire tracks again. Squatting, he drew a diagram in the dirt. The only vehicle he couldn't account for was the sand truck, one in the long anonymous succession of trucks feeding the piles. He thought for a moment, rubbing his sandpapery jaw.

"It's a longshot, but we might as well try it."

He drove back to the payloader. The mixing tank, at

the center of the great spiderweb, continued to be fed, to revolve, to disgorge. The landscaping and finishing crews were coming in to park their working vehicles and go home. The hot plant would go on working as long as it had daylight. A new load of sand was being dumped at the far side of the pile.

Climbing into the cab, Shayne told Benjamin, "Let's rotate. Get some of the new sand that's come in in the last half hour."

In the mouth of the culvert, Werner was making plans. The police had two dead men and a dead girl. That would keep them busy for hours. But they wouldn't be here all night. Werner was more worried about Benjamin and Vaughan. And he was worried about Downey. He could see Downey's car outside the control trailer, but Downey himself must be off with the other cops, trying to make sense of the multiple shootings. Like Benjamin and Vaughan, he would be looking for two things—a Styrofoam box and Werner.

Werner was lying almost in the water, so he wouldn't show up if anybody looked in the opposite end. The plan he settled on finally was to wait until just before daylight, if he could hold still that long. The lights would be on tonight, but they wouldn't reach to the far side of the sand pile. He had been counting loads. Only one more load had been dropped on top of the cooler. It would be easy digging. He couldn't hope to get home with the money tonight. He had to do it in stages. He would take it out through the culvert, bury it in the woods, marking the spot well, and come back for it later.

Downey would be just as baffled by these events as everybody else. Werner now knew that in smartness and toughness he was Downey's equal, if not his superior. All he lacked was experience, and he was getting that fast. With Pam dead—

And it really hit him for the first time. She actually was dead, all over, from the crown of her head to her toes. They had made love for the last time. They had been antagonists all along, even more so at the end. They had both changed under pressure. It would have been interesting to see which one ended up with the money.

He thought it would be safe now to doze a little. He was starting a long, hard period of waiting. The rhythmic clanking was more and more soothing. The payloader lunged, swung, tipped, and came back. Suddenly Werner snapped awake. It was changing position.

It maneuvered around the circle, where it seemed to hesitate for an instant; then it attacked. Instead of starting at shoulder level, the bucket dropped to the ground and made its first gouge there. It came up and around. Werner watched, more and more appalled. He had lined up the spot carefully so he would know where to dig. And it had planted itself at that exact spot.

His head whirling, he put on the yellow hat and dropped from the culvert. If the money didn't come out in the first bite, it was sure to come in the second or third, and he knew one thing for certain—he couldn't just sit there and watch. He had to do something. At the hot plant, sand from the bin drained steadily onto the bottom-most scoops of the belt. He had no idea how long the bin took to empty. He had to be there when the cooler dropped out. There was enough confused movement around and beneath the mixer so that he might be able to knock it off the belt without being seen.

As long as he was moving, he had a place in the pattern. He would become conspicuous the instant he stopped. He slowed down, and he was fifteen feet from the belt when there was an interruption in the smooth flow of sand. The cooler broke out of the mouth of the hopper.

Each segment of the belt slanted in toward the center to hold the sand. The cooler rode upward serenely, moving surprisingly fast. Werner had started running, but by the time he was in position, it was already inches out of reach.

The aperture in the tank's face was twenty-five feet from the ground. Without stopping to think, Werner leaped on the belt and scrambled up on all fours, pedaling hard. He gained a yard, slipped, and lost it again. He clawed upward, touching the cooler for an instant and knocking it off center. The dolphin on the lid seemed to be sneering at him. He drove again, and his foot went through the sand and caught between two of the V-shaped segments.

He tried to kick free, losing more ground. There were less than three feet to go now. He reached out desperately, and his fingers again grazed the Styrofoam. But it was firmly lodged, and it rode on to the top, tilted, and went in.

Werner's car was still there, near the pickup and the bodies, but no Werner. Downey looked for Benjamin and found him where he was supposed to be, up in his payloader. Mike Shayne was with him! Downey tried to find out from the sheriff's people what the idea was, what they were trying to do, but they didn't know much. Somebody thought there had been a kidnapping; that was the rumor that was going around. Downey's own status was a trifle uncertain. True, Larry Canada was one of his specialties, but he hadn't cleared it with anybody, and about all he could do was hang on the edge and listen.

Too many stimuli were crowding in on Downey at once, and his circuits were overloaded. People were running. He saw Werner first, in a hard hat, then above him on the belt the Styrofoam cooler, the money. It would be gone in another minute. Dumb, dumb. The kid had been focusing so hard on that box that when he saw it on the belt he climbed up and went after it. What if he did knock it off? From the beginning, Downey had known he couldn't afford to let Werner go in for questioning because he would surely answer those questions. Names would be named. This was trouble, real trouble.

Instead of moving toward the belts like everybody else, Downey stepped backward into the lee of the power cart. His gun had jumped into his hand.

One of the payloaders was swinging. The money dropped into the asphalt, and for an instant Downey thought Werner was going in after it, which would have solved that particular problem. One foot was tangled. He was face down, holding on with his full strength. He went into the hole in the face-plate, around the roller, and a second later he came back out on the underside of the belt, upside down. Somebody finally punched the right button and the belt stopped.

Werner was dangling twenty feet in the air. The payloader started a quick maneuver to get the bucket beneath him. Downey gave one look in both directions, half turned, and shot Werner off the belt.

The trapped foot pulled free when it took the full weight of Werner's body, and he fell into the gears.

Chapter 20

The gears had to be disassembled to get Werner out. No attempt was made to recover the beer cooler, for the Styrofoam would have disintegrated the instant it hit the hot oil. The next morning when the gears were reassembled and the hot plant resumed operation, the box and whatever had been inside it would be paved into the next stretch of highway.

The parents of the dead flag girl, in West Palm Beach, were notified of their daughter's death. They refused to believe it because their daughter, unquestionably alive, had just walked into the house. Other pieces dropped into place. Canada, who had spent the day in the van, was shown the bullet-ridden portable toilet. He loosened his neck inside his collar and gave Shayne a look of grudging respect. The muffled radio on the closed toilet seat had taken three slugs. If, instead of the radio, Canada had been sitting there, all three would have gone in near the base of his spine.

"You figured that one out, Shayne," he said. "Funny—I never thought Lou was that much of a threat. I thought he took it out on the golf balls and the tennis balls."

Shayne met him by arrangement the following morning outside the County Courthouse on East Flagler, where the bids on the Everglades spur were to be opened at nine. Having had a night to think over his predicament, Canada was experiencing more complicated feelings. It was no longer a simple matter of being glad he was alive.

"I've heard from a few people, Shayne. They put up some of that million, and the idea is, they want it back."

"Too bad. You may have to go into Chapter Eleven."

"Go bankrupt? Well, yeah, but these people, twenty cents on the dollar is not the way they like to get paid. I went along with your idea because I expected to recover that money. Hell, when that series of Rourke's gets rolling, I'll be spending most of my time in courtrooms. I'll need it for legal fees."

"Sorry, Larry. I never promised I could keep everything under control. There were too many wild cards, deuces and threes and one-eyed Jacks. What did you have for breakfast?"

Canada gave him a savage look. "I ate my normal breakfast. What do you think, I'm going on a diet because things haven't been breaking right?"

He walked away, the back of his neck red with anger. Shayne and Frieda found places in the chamber where the bids would be opened. Rourke gave Shayne a two-fingered salute. The media people clotted around Canada, but Rourke left him alone, having had his interview the day before. It had lasted six hours, and Rourke had been up most of the night writing an insider's view of the carnage at Homestead, and the next article in the highway series. Both his city editor and managing editor had come to the bid-opening because Rourke had promised more fireworks. All the TV channels had sent units.

Philip Gold, the Highway Commissioner, looking nearly as dapper as usual, arrived with a small staff. As he passed Shayne and Frieda, they caught a strong wash of perfume, a musky fragrance that wouldn't have seemed out of place on a bull moose. Frieda whispered, "He must want us to love him in spite of everything."

Gold took his place at the front of the chamber and asked if there were any last-minute bids. Parties of technicians from all the big contracting firms, including Canada's, had been busy in the corridor, scribbling changes and making their final quotes. The envelopes were hastily sealed. Canada's, as usual, came up last. Canada himself was sitting back, smiling. As everybody knew, his instinct was infallible. He invariably guessed right and gave the lowest bid by a narrow margin.

Gold put on heavy glasses and took a letter opener out of an attaché case. Everybody involved in the process began writing furiously as he opened each envelope and read out the figure. The bids, as always, varied so widely that the estimators seemed to be bidding on different jobs. Finally only two bidders were left to be heard from. One was a large Georgia firm, B. and B. Contractors, which had made a number of attempts to break into Florida highways and had invaria-

bly been beaten back. Gold's hands, as he arranged
the envelopes, were concealed behind a low rail, and
he managed to substitute a different envelope for B.
and B. Rourke and Shayne, however, had come early
to position a mirror above and behind him, high up to
the right of the flag. It was the action in this mirror
that the TV cameras were recording. Gold's attaché
case was open beside him. He read out a figure. There
was a murmur in the room. So far B. and B. had it,
with only Canada still to be heard from. Again Gold
did a sleight of hand with several envelopes hidden in
his case, all sealed, all identical except for the bids inside. Shayne had seen these envelopes before, when
Canada gave them to Gold at the meeting in the construction trailer. The letter opener snicked. Gold called
out a figure. By several tens of thousands, it was
higher than the one from the Georgia firm.

The room was absolutely still.

"It appears that B. and B. is low bidder," Gold announced, peering over his glasses. "Am I correct, gen-
tlemen? I therefore award B. and B. the contract. Con-
gratulations. I hope this leads to a long and fruitful
association."

The unopened envelopes were cleverly slipped back
in his attaché case, and the lid snapped shut. Canada
leaped to his feet, nearly purple.

"You double-crossing fink! You bastard! You cheap
kike! You think you're going to get away—"

His hand came up. There was a gun in it.

Shayne caught the arm and forced it down. "No,
Larry. Not today."

Canada threw himself from side to side. A vein like
a rope was beating in his temple. Others sprang to
help, but Shayne had the fat man under control. Gold
had dropped out of view as abruptly as if he had actually

been shot. Frieda reached across for the attaché case, containing the evidence of the fraudulent bidding. When the gun dropped, Canada's fierceness and fury went with it. His free hand came up to claw at his chest. He gurgled unpleasantly and slumped to the floor like an emptying grain sack.

A dirty youth in work jeans pushed through the crowd. "Are you Mike Shayne? Can you come quick?"

Shayne signaled to Rourke. Frieda's van was nearest, and they went in that.

"I was beginning to worry about you," Rourke said, getting in. "Because this has been one of your sloppiest efforts, you know that? Not that I'm complaining. Canada gave me some marvelous stuff, and I think those shenanigans with the bids may kill the Everglades link—put it off, anyway. So the paper's going to be more friendly when I go in to negotiate my next raise. However—"

"However what? You didn't really expect we'd put Canada in jail?"

"No, I guess not. A heart attack's almost as good. You stage-managed that nicely. How did you know Gold was planning to dump him?"

"Canada's hot this morning. And we know Gold— he was bound to try to make money out of it and close a deal with somebody else. A heart attack? I had my hand on his chest, and his heart beat seemed pretty good. But when he gets up off the floor, he's going to be hungry. He ate too much for breakfast, but it's almost time for a midmorning stack. He eats under pressure, and the pressure is going to be steady from now on. It's a stretched-out version of capital punishment. Now what else is bothering you?"

"You know what is bothering me. The money.

That's going to be the most expensive mile in Interstate history. When I saw that cooler go in— You've never been that careless before, Mike. I admit, I wouldn't have done it any better, but I've come to expect a little more efficiency from you."

Frieda, at the wheel, was smiling. "Thirsty, Tim? Have a beer."

"What are you talking about? I'm under pressure, too, but I don't drink beer under pressure. I'm more inclined to drink whiskey."

"Wouldn't a cold beer taste good right now? It's Miller's in cans. There's a cooler back of your seat."

Rourke's mouth opened. He looked from Frieda to Shayne. They were both laughing.

"No," Rourke said firmly. "Goddamn it, no. I saw that box go up the belt with my own eyes. 'Wallace for President,' without the W. That Goddamn stoned dolphin."

He waved in disgust. "All right, all right. You fooled me completely, but I wasn't the only one. When did you do it?"

"No problem," Shayne said. "We had most of the day, while you were talking to Canada. Those coolers are pretty standard. We weren't looking for any particular sticker, so long as we got them in pairs. Side by side, they weren't exactly identical, but nobody made the comparison. We put phone books in one, and that was the one that went into the asphalt. Benjamin made the switch in the parking lot when he came back from the rest area."

Rourke had twisted in his seat and unclamped the lid of the Styrofoam box. He lifted out the shallow compartment with its three cans of beer.

"My, my," he said. "Isn't it lovely?" He picked out several packages of hundreds, and let them spill slowly back. "A king's ransom. What are you going to do with it? Do I get a chance to vote? Keep it, Mike! Hell," he said in growing excitement, "you've been knocking your head against walls so long— Who does it belong to? A bunch of hoodlums! Turn it in, it'll disappear in the general fund the way those phone books disappeared in the asphalt. You deserve it. Nobody'll ever know. They all think it went in the Goddamn road."

"It's a lot of money," Shayne said. "We're thinking of setting up a foundation."

"The Mike Shayne Foundation," Rourke said promptly, "Mike Shayne, chief beneficiary. I'm for that."

Shayne shook his head. "Funded by the organized criminals of Miami. I want to set up a system of benefits for the victims. The people who get shot in the stick-ups. Hospital bills for people who get mugged. Reimbursement for thefts."

"I see it," Rourke said sadly, replacing the lid. "It's a nice idea, very poetic. And I can't even print the story. But it reassures me. I really did think you were slipping."

"What other loose ends are you worrying about?"

"The Eddie Maye thing. Money there, too. I missed your briefing, but you did say, didn't you, that Eddie was out collecting money the night he was killed? What happened to it? And there's one major character still unaccounted for. Mike, this isn't a criticism, you know that. Two groups of people, and you certainly disposed of the big majority. But you said at one point that Eddie Maye was being followed by a cop, and as I understand it, you were aiming at a cop in a couple of those moves. Well, he's still walking around with a gun and a badge, and I admit it bothers me."

Frieda started to speak, but Rourke rode her down.

"And I'm willing to swear that somebody put a bullet in that kid before he dropped off that belt. You didn't see it from up above in the payloader. I saw him jerk. That was a bullet," he insisted. "I suppose he's too mangled up now to be sure, but I'm going on claiming he was shot. There were all kinds of cops out there, all of them with guns. Our cop didn't want the kid to be taken, the only one left who could nail him for kidnapping and murder."

"I have a list of every police officer on the scene at the time," Shayne said. "Believe it or not, there were sixteen. All right, which one? That's why I leaned so hard on the money Eddie Maye was collecting for De-Luca. I said it could go as high as a hundred thousand. I pulled that figure out of the air. We have no way of knowing. But people who are in the business of making illegal loans need some system for carrying money so they won't be hit before they can get it to the bank. Eddie had an old Volkswagen. He went on driving it long after you'd expect him to trade it in. Maybe that was because he'd had some custom body work done on the car."

Rourke said slowly, "I think I'm beginning to see—"

"Like an extra compartment across the back of the trunk. In a bug, that's under the dashboard. A concealed opening from the driver's side so he could slip in packages of bills. And if he was making the rounds that night, putting the arm on people for the DeLuca campaign, that's where it would go. Eddie's body turned up a day later, but where's the car? That's the question I left open when I was explaining this stuff to the cops. Maybe the kidnappers were seen in that car, and they decided they had to get rid of it."

"Then it's at the end of some swamp road somewhere."

"If so, it won't help us tie off the last loose end. A better place would be a junkyard. One of those standard VW's is cannibalized in a matter of weeks. Engine, rear end, transmission—pretty soon nothing's left but the frame, and they scrap that. The point is—"

"I see the point," Rourke said. "Finally. Nobody knows where that VW is except the guy who put it there."

"And he hasn't cleared anything out of this so far. He knows I was guessing about the hundred thousand, but wouldn't he want to check? I called all the main junkyards and said if anybody came in to look at stripped VW's, to notify me at the courthouse, and every sighting was worth fifty bucks."

They had crossed the Miami River and now they were moving north on the drive. Where it dead-ended, they circled on side streets, coming back under the expressway to the largest of the riverside junkyards. The youth who had come for Shayne was waiting at the gate. He pointed. They drove down a wide alley between junked cars toward a man who was examining a VW without headlights or front bumper. Shayne picked a gun off the floor.

Frieda stopped the van, and Shayne stepped down. The man turned.

"Downey," Shayne said, "I had an idea it might turn out to be you."

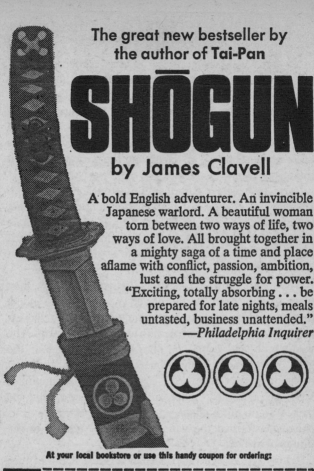

THE
GARGOYLE
CONSPIRACY

A novel by
Marvin H. Albert

A bomb explodes in the Rome airport, leaving shreds of human flesh strewn about the wreckage. But it was nothing compared to what was to come. It was only the first step of a master terrorist who combined irresistible sexual seduction, all-powerful Arab oil money, an army of terrorist assassins and the latest in sophisticated weaponry in a plot to assassinate the American Secretary of State.

A great new thriller guaranteed to hold you on excitement's edge from the first explosive page to the ultimate shattering shock.

A Dell Book $1.95   (5239-02)

DECEMBER 11, 1944 . . . U.S.S. *Candlefish,* submarine on wartime patrol, mysteriously lost. at Latitude 30 in the Pacific. All hands perish, except for one survivor.

OCTOBER 5, 1974 . . . Six hundred miles northwest of Pearl Harbor, a submarine surfaces in front of a Japanese freighter. It is the *Candlefish,* in perfect working order fully outfitted down to steaks in the freezer yet without a trace of life aboard.

In Washington, D.C., a naval intelligence officer is convinced that the *Candlefish* was the victim of another Devil's Triangle, and convinces his superiors to send it on a voyage retracing her route of thirty years before in the hope of uncovering whatever fearful force lies in wait at Latitude 30.

Only when the sub is well out to sea, with no turning back, do he and the rest of the crew begin to suspect why the *Candlefish* has come back from a watery grave, and what that means to every living soul aboard.

GHOSTBOAT

by George E. Simpson and Neal R. Burger